A Stack of Sawbucks

In This Series

That First Heady Burn

True Vermilion

The Dark Shill

A Stack of Sawbucks

The Hillside Roble

The Peroxide Pomp

The Incidental Twin

Brawl in Bardo

The Window-Shade Job

The Convenient Patsy

The Artisanal Grifter

Shrink in the Shadows

Project Chartreuse

From a Desert Playa

The Tired Canary

A Desperate Frame-up

Trail of the Blue Agave

The Saucer-Heads

A Stack of Sawbucks

A Stack of Sawbucks

George Bixley

DAGMAR MIURA

LOS ANGELES

Published by Dagmar Miura
Los Angeles
www.dagmarmiura.com

A Stack of Sawbucks

First published 2018

ISBN: 978-1-942267-65-2

Slater hated the freaking Miracle Mile, a tract of dense apartment houses built in the 1920s, when no one had a car—there was never anywhere to park. Cruising past the address his business partner, Max, had summoned him to, Slater gave up trolling for a street space and pulled into a lot behind an office supply store on Wilshire Boulevard. There was no parking attendant per se, but a guy wearing a red polo shirt with the company's logo on it sat on a stool outside the back door to the store, watchful. Slater locked up the Thunderbird and strolled inside, amid the stationery and electronics, then out the front door to the boulevard, and back around onto the side street.

Walking up the block, he took his time—it

was mid-summer, the hottest part of the day, and Slater always wore jeans. He never bothered with hats or sunscreen, as he had his father's dark Latin American coloring, purpose-built for sunny climes like Los Angeles.

Max had asked him here to consult on a case that he had framed as a "haunted apartment." Max was reasonable, even though Slater regularly wanted to punch him in the face, so there had to be more to it than high-strung people with creaky floors in a century-old building. The questionable part was that Max had a personal connection to the case, which was risky in their business—Max was a licensed PI, and Slater did investigative dirty work for an insurance company.

"The tenants are my maybe-girlfriend's sister and her boyfriend," Max had explained. "I really like this woman. She's smart, and nice, you know?"

"I know what nice is like, sure," Slater had told him, "but what worries me is that you seem smitten—talking about her personality, not her hair color or her hot curves."

"Not everyone is a piece of meat like the guys you date," Max said.

"I don't objectify every guy—just the ones I sleep with, and the ones I need to slap around."

Max threw up his hands. "That's practically every guy you meet."

Walking up on the apartment, Slater double-checked the address on his phone. It was a bulky redbrick building on a corner lot. Between the two wings, on the walkway in to the entrance, was a courtyard with an old stone fountain and lush landscaping. Slater admired the sword ferns and the *polyanthum* jasmine on the way in. That was plain lazy landscaping, planting those. They sucked up too much water and grew like weeds, but they did smell amazing in the spring when they bloomed.

There was no list of tenants at the door, just a brass plate inscribed with the name of the building: THE CAMELLIA. He hadn't seen any camellias in the courtyard, or even out on the parkway along the street, where there were bauhinias, so new that they still had support posts around their slender trunks. The name probably dated to the original construction, when the neighborhood would have been more upscale. The front door had a lock, he noticed, but it was open today, and inside was a concierge desk that probably hadn't been staffed since the 1940s. The lobby hadn't been remodeled either, although the paint job was recent, and the thick red carpet was new. Treading back toward the elevator, he went up the wide stairs to the third floor, finding the door to 302 down a corridor brightly lit by the windows along one side that overlooked the entry courtyard and its fountain.

Slater rapped at the door, and a woman soon pulled it open. Max and a guy were standing inside behind her.

"Slater," Max called, stepping toward the door. He was a thick man, with a little gut hanging over his belt, but he looked sharp in a summery seersucker suit, his weapon bulging under one arm, the holster strap visible.

"I just got here myself," Max said. "This is Jessica, and her boyfriend, Mike."

Both were in their mid-twenties, and Jessica looked athletic, dressed in stretchy jeans and a billowy top, her African hair tied back in long braids. Mike was tall, and dark too, maybe Middle Eastern, and inadvertently hot in that way that straight guys sometimes were.

"It's warm out there," Mike said, after Slater had introduced himself. "Do you want a drink? I've got cold Kronenbourg."

"Not for me," Slater said.

"Are you sure? It's Sunday."

Slater glared at him. What was wrong with people? "I said no."

Mike shrugged and walked into the kitchen, past a small dining table, the fridge and countertops visible through the open archway. Slater watched him go, assessing the pleasing fit of his cargo shorts.

Slater caught Jessica's eye and gestured to the

suitcases parked beside the front door. "Going somewhere?" he demanded.

Jessica arched her eyebrows, giving him a subtle once-over. "We're traveling tonight, but that's no concern of yours—it's not related to our ghost problem." She stepped over to the sofa.

The furniture was midcentury modern, which looked good on the wooden floor, the narrow boards and dark stain implying it was as old as the building itself. Beyond the sofa were a couple of easy chairs, backs to the corner windows, and a plaster faux fireplace, de rigueur in any dwelling of this vintage.

Slater joined her, dropping into one of the chairs with a view of the space. Beyond the kitchen a hallway led farther back, but the weirdest feature was in this room, near the kitchen—a curving staircase with no handrails that dead-ended at the flat white ceiling. Mike and Jessica had lined the dark-wood steps with framed photos and rows of books.

Max came over and sat in the black Barcelona chair, leaning forward, eager and attentive, like a kid who wanted to earn a merit badge.

"I've heard about Max," Jessica said, eyeing Slater, "but not about you."

"We work together," Max said quickly, but Jessica was focused on Slater.

"We share resources," Slater said, "although

we're usually working different cases."

"Slater has saved my butt several times," Max said. "We met when he poached the daughter of my former employer as a client."

"Sounds juicy," Jessica said, reclining on the sofa.

Slater shot Max a murderous look. That's not how it had happened. He wanted to punch that grin off his face, but he forced himself to swallow his ire.

Slater eyed Jessica. "Why did you ask for Max's help?"

Mike returned, beer bottles in hand, and gave one to Max before joining Jessica on the sofa.

"Well," Jessica began, "at night we've started to hear ghosts. We don't know why it began all of a sudden, but it's upsetting. We call it ghosts, but we're not sure what it is." She shrugged helplessly. "My sister said she was dating a guy who knew about security."

"That is my field," Max said, gesturing with the bottle of Kronenbourg in his thick fingers. "What do you hear, exactly?"

"Moaning," Mike said, "like someone's in pain. My great uncle was on morphine at the end of his life, and when it was wearing off, he sounded exactly the same. It's horrible."

"And rushing water," Jessica added. "I got up a few times to see if a pipe had burst, or the dishwasher was flooding. There's a crying baby sometimes too."

"The baby is definitely the freakiest," Mike said. "It stabs you in the heart. It must be an instinct kicking in. Like nature telling you, 'Take care of this.'"

"It only happens at night?" Max asked.

"Late at night," Jessica said. "Like, three or four."

"Where does the sound come from?" Slater asked.

She looked to Mike. "We both thought it felt like it's in the middle of the bedroom, and in the middle of this room too when you come in. It's like it's all around."

"When you stand near the wall," Mike said, "it sounds like it's closer. But it can't be outside the wall—Sixth Street is on that side, and the kitchen is on the other. It just kind of fills the room."

"The counterintuitive thing is that it's not really scary," Jessica said. "Just creepy. Neither one of us thinks it's really a ghost. That's why we called Max instead of those ghost-hunter types with the night-vision cameras."

"If it's not a ghost, what do you think it is?" Slater asked.

Jessica pursed her lips. "My grandmother grew up in the South before the civil rights era. She said one of the things the Klan used to keep black folks in line was ghost stories, and ghost rides on horses late at night."

"Keep people afraid, and they won't make waves," Mike said glumly.

"But why would anyone be doing that to us?" Jessica demanded.

Max turned to Slater. "What do you think?"

"Do you know any of your neighbors?" Slater asked.

Mike shook his head. "We only have one shared wall, at the back, in the bathroom. Two of our walls are on the outside of the building, and the fourth one is the hallway."

Slater nodded, glancing around the space, arranging it in his mind. "Have you ever seen anyone with a baby?"

"The building isn't really for families," Mike said. "Mostly it's people our age—singles or couples, transplants from other places."

And totally Anglo, Slater thought, although they probably didn't even notice.

"The whole neighborhood is like that," Max said. "People start out here and move on when the lack of parking gets annoying."

"Can we look around?" Slater asked.

Jessica rose, sweeping her arm at the room in tacit assent.

Slater walked into the kitchen, then down the

hall to the bedroom. These people were tidy—the bed was made, the closet doors closed, and nothing was on the floor. The windows faced Sixth Street, which would be noisy at night. At the end of the hall was the bathroom, with new tile but an old-school pedestal sink and a vintage tub.

Max stepped into the bathroom behind him. "The wet wall is the one shared with the neighbor."

"That can't be where the noise is coming from," Slater said, and followed him to the front door, then out into the hall. At the end was a big multipaned window, facing the side street, with a fire escape landing just outside, the narrow metal stairs running down. He turned back toward the elevator.

"The main stairs come up right about where the wet wall is," Slater said. The hallway continued beyond, with two apartment doors on either side.

Max stepped toward the stairs. "So Mike is right—there's just one neighbor."

"Except the ones above and below," Slater said. "Did you notice the dead staircase in the middle of their apartment?"

"Hard to miss," Max said.

Back inside, they found Mike and Jessica standing in the living room.

Slater gestured to the staircase. "Stairs to nowhere. Did anyone ever explain that?"

Jessica folded her arms. "The manager said this was originally a two-level apartment, but sometime in the 1960s they subdivided it. The stairs were too ornate and beautiful to destroy, so they left them and just covered over the ceiling."

"It makes sense they did that," Max said. "This neighborhood isn't as glamorous as it was in the 1920s. In a declining area you'd want smaller units and more of them."

Jessica frowned. "You think the neighborhood's in decline?"

"Not now," Max said quickly. "Back then."

Slater stood next to the stairs, looking up. Most of the ceiling was original plaster, coved at the corners, but at the top of the stairs was the outline of where the hole to the upper floor had been, covered now in newer drywall.

"Have you ever tried to push through it?" Slater asked.

"Never," Mike said flatly.

"Is it possible that all the noise is coming from here?"

Jessica shook her head. "It doesn't seem like that when it's happening. It feels like it's right in the room, and right in the bedroom, not near the stairs."

"We do hear the people up there," Mike said, "but it's the sound of furniture being moved around, and heavy stuff dropping, and hammering.

They must be crafty. I never met them, but I've complained to the management office about it when they're working late at night."

Slater stepped around behind the stairs and pulled open the narrow door there. Jackets hung in front, and behind them, under the descending stairs, storage boxes were stacked.

Stepping back around to face the tenants, he said, "If you're hearing noises late at night, I want to be here."

"I can give you the keys," Mike said, glancing at Jessica. "Be here as much as you like. We're leaving in a couple of hours. You can both stay, if you want."

Jessica looked dubious. "Are you sure you need to do that? I thought you'd have some idea about where it's coming from, and what's going on."

Slater put his hands on his hips. "We need to hear it ourselves before we can advise you, or take any action."

She frowned. "I don't know. Do either of you smoke?"

"We're not going to mess up your stuff," Slater snapped.

Max put a hand on Slater's shoulder and eyed Jessica. "Nobody's going to smoke," he said gently. "We're professionals—we do stakeouts and surveillance all the time."

"You're not going to cook, are you? We keep the kitchen vegan."

"Huh. Small vegan world," Slater said.

Her eyebrows shot up. "You're vegan?"

"Am I not bougie-looking enough to be?" Slater said intently, his voice rising.

"We won't be cooking here," Max said quickly. "We'll just be hanging out for a few hours, and hopefully we'll hear what you've been hearing."

Jessica sighed. "I guess that's OK."

"I'll get the keys," Mike said, and went down the hall.

Max turned to Jessica. "Where are you headed?" he asked affably.

"Back to New York," she said. "Visiting family. Just five days."

Mike returned, handing Max a pair of keys on a loop of string.

"At least it's summer, so the weather will be decent," Max said, pocketing them.

"It's actually not," Jessica said. "It's ninety-five every day, and humid like the bottom of a swimming pool."

Slater scoffed. "I can see why you'd move out here."

"Have fun, anyway," Max said. "We'll let you know what we find out."

Slater followed him out the door. They were both silent as they walked down the stairs to the lobby, then out through the greenery and past the fountain. Once they reached the sidewalk, Max stopped on the grassy parkway, next to the tightly parked cars.

"Are they crazy?" he asked.

"If there really is all that noise going on, someone's trying to get them out," Slater said.

"That's what I thought too. It seems odd, though, because it's a rental building. I could see it happening in a condo, where someone wants to buy next door and expand their space."

"What about the landlord? It's hard to get rid of tenants who are clean and pay the rent on time, but it's not unheard of to push people out so you can jack the rent to market value."

"They told me they've only been there a year," Max said, "so they're already paying close to market."

Slater looked up at the building, following the fire escape as it zigzagged up to the fourth floor. "I wonder if it's one of the neighbors? We should look at the apartments above and below."

"Good idea," Max said. "You take the second floor; I'll go up to the fourth."

They went back inside and up the stairs. The second floor had the same hallway as on the third, where Mike and Jessica lived, with the same big window onto the fire escape. The door to 202 matched the one to 302—the same orange paint, glassy peephole, standard lock. Slater went back down to the lobby and waited for Max out on the sidewalk.

When Max came out, he was flushed, his eyes bright, and he stood close, speaking in a hushed tone. "Whoever lives in 402 put in a majorly complex deadbolt, and there's a camera in the peephole."

"Seriously?" Slater said. "The door to 202 has a standard hardware-store lock, the same as Mike and Jessica's."

"I took a photo of it," Max said, and when he saw Slater's eyes narrow, added, "Don't worry—I pretended I was looking out at the fire escape and futzing with my phone so that it didn't look like surveillance." Pulling open his jacket, he fished the device out of his inner pocket.

"Is your car nearby?" Slater asked, glancing up at the building.

"Good idea." Max gestured up the block, and they soon came to the familiar matte-gray Challenger, with its dark-tinted windows, parked at the curb.

Slater climbed in the passenger door as Max went around to the driver's side.

Leaning toward him, Max pulled up a photo on his phone. "See the crazy shape of the keyhole?"

It was indeed unusual, Slater saw, four-sided and oblong and pinched in the middle. The plate surrounding it looked heavy-duty, and at the top Slater could make out a stylized character etched into the gray metal: Ⲉ.

"I know that logo," Slater said. "Masamune." He pulled out his own phone and found the manufacturer's website, handing it to Max.

"High-security deadbolts," Max read. "Titanium strike plate … it says the keys are impossible to copy."

"When you see a Masamune, you don't try to go through it. It's easier to get a circular saw and cut through the wall instead."

"If this is the same model," Max said, scrolling through the page, "it costs eight hundred bucks."

Slater looked out at the sidewalk, absently checking out a guy passing by. "So the question is, why would a rented apartment need an eight-hundred-dollar unbreakable lock on the door? Maybe I'll go back and have a look."

Max handed back his phone. "I wouldn't— there's more. Mounted just past the stairwell is a camera, facing down the hall toward 402. I know it's not the landlord's because there isn't one on the third floor, and there's no surveillance at all in the lobby."

"There wasn't one on the second floor either. So whoever lives in 402 has two cameras covering that hallway. What are they so worried about?"

"On my way in today I had a look around,

and went by the management office," Max said. "The sign on the door says it's not open on the weekend, but I can go tomorrow and try to find out who's living there."

"Good." Slater nodded. "I'm going to sleep here. Do you have a stepladder?"

"At home, sure."

"Bring it over here tonight. I'll be back in a few hours."

"For what?"

"I'm going to get that camera. Give me the keys to Jessica and Mike's."

Max dug in his jacket pocket and handed them over. "Call me when you get here."

Slater pocketed the keys and climbed out, walking up the block toward Wilshire and the office supply store, eying Max's car as it cruised past. Slater went to the street entrance of the store and strolled through to the parking lot.

As he unlocked the door of his Thunderbird, the attendant called to him, "All that time inside and you didn't buy anything?"

"What, you have a stopwatch for every car in the lot?" Slater demanded.

"Only the ones that stand out. What year is that baby?"

"It's a '78," Slater said, and climbed in. That was the problem with driving a classic car—it drew more attention than someone in his business needed, and he usually had to park out of view of where he was going. But he loved it, loved the throaty engine and the cherry interior.

Navigating the side streets of the neighborhood, he crossed Wilshire and went south to Olympic, following it downtown to the Fashion District, where he and Max shared an office. Surrounded by wholesalers selling fabric and zippers and myriad other clothing-industry supplies, the high-rise that contained their office housed mostly sewing factories. Because it was Sunday, the surface lot across the street where he parked was almost abandoned, the attendant's booth shuttered. Slater opened the trunk of the Thunderbird to retrieve his satchel, slinging it on his shoulder, then slammed it again, heading across to his building. On a workday there were always day laborers hanging around the entrance and the lobby, waiting for sewing and cutting gigs, but today it was quiet.

Their office was up nine floors, tucked around behind the elevator shaft, just three rooms—an office for each of them and a small reception space, with an unused desk and a hat rack that for months had held only an unclaimed umbrella. Slater felt a twinge of guilt at the sight of the barren desk—the resident potted *Pothos* had finally died. Maybe there hadn't been enough light to keep it alive. Max's office had a window, but this one and Slater's didn't. In his own space he'd put up a faded thrift-store painting of artichokes in a bowl. Those, at least, he couldn't kill.

Sitting at his desk and swinging his boots up onto it, staring at the artichokes and not seeing them, he thought through his plan for the evening. Not finding any holes in it, he pulled out his phone and checked on Conrad, his idiot ex-boyfriend, who'd kicked him to the curb after a brief intense relationship. The very sight of him was infuriating, but he kept contact with Conrad because he was a cop, and had access to resources that Slater needed. When they'd been together, back when things had still been good, Slater had slipped a hidden app onto his phone that relayed his location in real time. It was the idiot's own fault, letting Slater see the code he used to unlock it. You'd think a cop would be a little more security-conscious. Right now Conrad was drifting slowly along Sunset Boulevard in Echo Park. He must be on patrol, the freaking moron.

Slater killed the tracking app in disgust and pulled his feet off the desk, pushing Conrad out of his mind and turning to the safe he shared with Max. It was bolted to the floor in the corner of Slater's office, and he dialed in the combination, pulling open the heavy door and retrieving the gear he'd need tonight, loading it into his satchel and locking up again.

TWO

It was a long while until sundown, but it was easier to eat around here before heading back to the Miracle Mile and its dearth of parking. Not far away was a gritty pub, frequented by downtown residents, that incongruously served only vegan fare. Slater parked on the street and went in, ordering from the pub food menu at the bar.

"You want a beer with that?" the bartender asked.

"Just the grub." Having a beer right now didn't fit with his booze rules: he only drank alone when he was in for the night, or at least when the workday was over, and there was more to do. Conrad thought he drank too much, despite that being none of his freaking business. Slater was in control of it, had it figured out. And nobody was going to tell him what to do.

The pub wasn't busy yet, and Slater found a seat at a communal table, looking at his phone while he waited for his food. Mike and Jessica both had social media accounts, he found, and both were private, but some of their photos were visible. They seemed like ordinary twenty-somethings. Jessica appeared in a couple of photos with her acting class, and Mike's feed contained a mention of Tufts; maybe he'd gone to school there. When his food arrived, he pocketed his phone.

Launching into his burger, it felt like someone was watching him. It paid to be hyperalert sometimes in his work, but this time it wasn't a threat. A guy with his mousy brown hair in a natty pomp, sitting across the table and down a ways, seemed to be checking him out. Or maybe not—the guy had a motor-function problem, maybe CP, so it was hard to tell. Ignoring the ambiguity, Slater caught his eye and winked, double-clicking his tongue.

That got a reaction: the guy twitched more intently for a second, then spoke, his speech slightly distorted.

"Are you … flirting with me?"

"That depends," Slater said, raising his voice to be heard over the pub's music. "Does your disability have a cognitive component?"

The guy frowned. "Why does that … matter?"

"I don't want your mother bringing the cops to my door claiming I assaulted you."

He scoffed. "It's not cognitive. And why would you … bring my mother into it? She's not the boss of me. She lives in Orange County anyway."

"For that, she has my condolences," Slater said, taking another bite of his burger.

"I hate when people assume I'm slow just because I talk slow."

"Dude," Slater said intently, "I didn't make any assumptions about you. I didn't know—that's why I asked."

He nodded, looking a little sheepish.

"To answer your question: yes, I am flirting."

The guy shot him a wry smile. "I wish I could click my … tongue like you did."

"What's your name, son?"

"You're not that much older than me, you … condescending ass. It's Andy."

"Can I buy you a beer, Andy?"

"I don't drink, but you could take me home, and we could mess around."

Slater chuckled. "The direct approach. I respect that."

Andy raised his eyebrows, a subtle challenge.

"I live in Westlake," Slater said. "There's an elevator, but there are a few stairs to get to it."

"You can come to my place. I live right around the corner."

"Can I finish my burger first?"

"If you must," Andy said. "But make it … snappy."

Slater grinned and finished his food, then wiped his hands, scooting his chair away from the table. Andy rose, reaching for the walking sticks propped against the wall behind him, slipping his arms into the cuffs, grabbing the handles. Slater followed him out to the street. Watching him walk was a little unnerving, as he didn't look very stable, but Slater walked abreast, matching his pace, strolling leisurely up Spring Street and over to Broadway. Subtly checking him out, he saw that Andy had great musculature, in his upper body at least, and a nice butt.

A guy standing in a doorway pulled his attention away, asking, "Spare change?"

Slater met his eye and said flatly, "No."

After they'd passed, the homeless guy said, "Spaz," just loud enough to be heard.

Slater looked back, then turned to Andy. "Is that a slur?"

"Totally," he said.

Slater stopped. "That stupid fuck."

"I hear it every day," Andy said. "Just let it go."

Slater walked back toward the homeless guy, his fists balled at his sides. "You need to learn some manners," he said, approaching the doorway, and punched the guy in the face, fast and sharp, not hard enough to cause any damage, but nonetheless a clear message.

The guy spun around and darted out of the doorway. "What's your problem?" he shouted, backing away. "He's a spaz. That's all I said. Look at him."

Slater strode intently toward him, but the guy wasn't up for a scuffle, turning and loping away. Watching him, Slater stopped, and when the guy looked back, called after him, "Keep on running, chump."

A man and woman walking past gave Slater a wide berth, glancing furtively at him. He turned back, rejoining Andy, standing sideways now to watch, resting on his walking sticks.

"Why did you do that?" Andy demanded. "I don't need a freaking bodyguard."

Slater threw up his hands. "Doesn't that piss you off?"

"I can fight my own battles."

"I didn't do it for you. It's kind of what I do for a living, punching knuckleheads like him."

"I don't let it ... get under my skin," Andy said, gesturing with his stick.

"Well, I don't not let it get under my skin." He sighed. "Do you want me to leave?"

"I want you to come upstairs and get naked."

Slater grinned. "Good."

"I'm right here," Andy said, leading him a few paces to an entryway and punching the button to open the door.

Slater looked up at the facade. It was a loft building in a former warehouse. He'd seen it before, and knew it was a recent conversion, but he'd never been inside. He followed Andy into the elevator.

Andy's space was a roomy studio, with original wooden flooring, the atmospheric scuffs and stains of its former life varnished over and still visible. The warm light of the end of the day streamed in the big windows. They had lots of little panes in them, so they must be original too.

Slater stood between the bed and the windows as Andy propped his sticks against the wall next to his desk, which bore three computer monitors, dark now, and a couple of black plastic objects that looked like armored gloves.

"What are those?" Slater asked him, gesturing to the desk.

"Input devices for someone with crappy fine-motor skills," Andy said.

"You walk pretty well," Slater said, gesturing to the wheelchair that sat folded up in a corner. "Why do you have that?"

"I use it when my feet get too messed up." He moved closer to Slater, who put his arms around his waist and kissed him.

It took a bit of adjustment, getting used to Andy's taut muscles and random twitches, but it worked, connecting with him, his mouth warm and inviting. Slater felt his dick tightening in his jeans, and pulled Andy closer. Andy pulled back and sank onto the bed, and Slater followed, straddling him, unbuttoning his shirt, kissing his chest.

When Slater pulled off his own shirt, Andy said, "Stand up."

"Why?"

"So I can watch," he said, smirking at him.

Slater stood at the end of the bed, eyes locked on Andy's, and unbuckled his belt, then slowly unbuttoned his jeans. After he pulled off his boots, he slid his jeans down, exposing his raging woody.

Andy unzipped his pants. "You're so damn … hot," he said, grabbing his own cock.

"Do you want me to fuck you?" Slater said, kneeling on the bed and working his pants off.

"I do, but I'm not ready for that," Andy said. "I can fuck you, if you straddle me."

"That works," Slater said, and found a condom in the drawer that Andy pointed out. He worked Andy's cock until it was fully hard and rolled it onto him.

Straddling Andy, he slid down onto him, wincing at the intensity of it. Andy gasped and grabbed Slater's forearms, and as Slater built up a rhythm, Andy started pounding on Slater's thighs with his fists. Slater wasn't sure if it was intentional or involuntary, but in any case, Andy came, his arms flailing, his head arching back.

Climbing off, Slater lay beside him, kissing his neck, his nose in Andy's hair. He grabbed his own cock but Andy batted his hand away, stroking him until he came too.

Once he'd caught his breath, Andy said, "Could you grab a towel from the … bathroom?"

Slater got up and found one, handing it to him and stretching out again.

"I dig your pad," Slater said. "The high ceilings are great."

"I work here too, so I need the space."

"What do you do?"

"I'm something of a whiz with … computers."

"Are you, now. That doesn't sound egotistical at all."

Andy scoffed. "It's not egotistical if it's true."

"Do you do research? Maybe I could hire you to do some work."

"What kind of research?"

"It's all about information," Slater said, lacing his fingers into Andy's.

"So go to the freaking library."

"What would be useful to me is more like a virtual break and enter."

"That's illegal by definition," Andy said, turning to look at him. "But you're so hot, I'd try anything you said."

Slater stayed a while, enjoying the warmth of Andy's body. The last glow of daylight faded behind the towers of the Financial District looming beyond the tattersall windows. It was so great that this guy didn't need to chat, comfortable just to be here, with their bodies in proximity.

Finally Slater said, "I have to go. I'm working tonight."

"At least you won't be tense," Andy said, and rolled to the bedside, grabbing his phone. "Give me your number."

It had a heavy case that made it look like it could survive a bus rolling over it, and Andy tapped at the screen methodically as Slater got dressed, focusing on the oversize numeric keyboard, punching the numbers in slowly after Slater recited them.

Slater's phone buzzed in his pants, and he pulled it out. "Did you just text me? Where's 949?"

"That's me," Andy said.

"So I've got your number now too."

Andy looked up at him. "You gave me your real number."

"Of course I did," Slater snapped. "If I didn't want you to have it, I'd say so. I wouldn't lie about it."

"Maybe I spoke too soon. You're tense again."

Slater scoffed and let himself out, walking back to his car. It was almost dark but still warm, heat radiating from the concrete. Maybe he shouldn't have given Andy his number. The guy was hot, and Slater liked that he was a little brash. But he didn't want to get sticky—not with Andy, not with any guy.

Heading west on Olympic, Slater stopped in Koreatown at a strip-mall liquor store, scanning the aisles until he found the bourbon he liked. Usually he bought it in fifths, but he was staying at somebody else's house; he couldn't drink that much. Jessica had been leery of him even being there, but that was probably because she thought she had nice stuff, and that he'd steal from her. Pulling three pint bottles off the shelf, he took them to the till and waited as the clerk rang them up and slipped them into paper bags.

The next stop was quick, at a hardware store, where he had just one purchase to make: a plastic card with WET PAINT emblazoned in big red letters.

People in the Miracle Mile were home for the evening, it seemed, and after trolling several blocks for a street space, Slater finally found one big enough for the Thunderbird. It was far from the Camellia building, but at least he'd found it, and he deftly backed in. It was annoying to have to leave his wheels on the street all night, but this was a busy road, and he'd parked a few yards from a stoplight, which made it less likely that he'd get jacked. Before he climbed out, he texted Max:

I'm at Jessica and Mike's.

Opening the trunk, he packed his dark-blue gardening coveralls into his satchel, along with a pair of wiring pliers, a couple of screwdrivers, and one of the new pints of bourbon, then slung the bag over his shoulder, walking half a dozen blocks back to the hulking redbrick apartment house. With the electronic gear he'd taken from the office, the bag was heavy and bulky, but he knew he'd need all of it.

The entrance courtyard with the fountain was cooler at this hour than the street, with all the humid greenery. The front door was locked now, and he had to dig for the keys Mike had given Max. Upstairs at the door to 302 he knocked loudly and listened, just in case Mike and Jessica had missed their flight or changed their plans, but there was no sound, and when he twisted the key in the lock and pushed his way inside, the place was dark, the suitcases gone.

First he did a sweep of the apartment, flicking on the lights and looking in closets, pushing the clothes aside, pulling back the shower curtain, scanning any place a person could fit. Next he methodically photographed each room, from the middle and then standing in each corner. If things got messed up, he could use the photos to put everything back where it had been. The curving staircase to nowhere gave the room an odd vibe, he decided, but using the steps as bookshelves was a reasonable way to repurpose it. He wouldn't have torn out that beautiful polished wood either.

Satisfied, finally, he turned off the lights and pulled the drapes, then sank onto the sofa. The only light came from the hallway, through the slit at the bottom of the door, along with the constellation of LEDs on the video and audio components floating around the television set. Slater listened to the room, listened to the building. Under the muted traffic noise outside was a low hum, maybe an air-conditioning unit somewhere. It was noisier than his crummy apartment, which probably cost half as much, and the neighborhood was way too busy and urban to feel spooky, regardless of what the occupants had been hearing.

In his jeans his phone rang, jarring in the quiet dark room. He pulled it out and squinted at the screen; it was Max.

"Can you come down and get the ladder?"

Max said. "There's nowhere to park. I'm in the red zone right outside."

Slater trotted down, not bothering to lock the deadbolt behind him. At the corner was a little green truck that he'd never seen before, its flashers on. It had a dent or two and needed a paint job, but overall it was a gem. When he leaned into the open passenger window, sure enough, there was Max.

"Where did you get this sweet ride?" Slater demanded.

"I told you I had a pickup."

"You never told me it was a classic Courier. It's beautiful." Slater looked over the dashboard. "'74, maybe?"

"It's a '73."

"You've been holding out on me, partner."

Max chuckled. "Do you need a hand inside? I can park on Wilshire and walk back."

"No need, but let's talk in the morning. I was thinking—Jessica is pretty young. How old is her sister?"

"Old enough. Not that who I'm dating is any of your business." He jabbed his thumb at the rear window. "Would you grab the damn ladder before I get popped?"

Slater grinned and pulled the ladder out of the back. It was aluminum, lightweight enough that he could hike it up under one arm.

"Got it," he called, stepping back, and Max waved as he pulled away.

Walking back through the courtyard, he passed a woman on her way out, her hair short, earbuds in and wearing sweats. She greeted him perfunctorily, unsuspicious, even though he was a brown guy carrying a ladder at night in an Anglo neighborhood. It was probably typical of a building where people didn't stay very long; the tenants didn't know each other, and she assumed he belonged here.

Once he was inside, he propped the ladder against the wall beside the door, then experimented with leaving the bathroom light on, and then the one in the hall, finally settling on the kitchen light to cast just enough illumination into the living room. That beautiful golden pint had been waiting for him all this time, and he pulled it out of his satchel now, cracking the seal and taking a pull. The delicious nectar burned his palate, his throat, his belly, and he could feel his body start to relax with that first taste.

It was tempting to put on a podcast, but he needed to be able to hear the ghost; that was the whole point of being here. Instead he pulled his boots off and stretched out on the sofa, setting the pint bottle on the little Persian rug spread under the coffee table. Loosening his belt, he tried to shift into a better position. That was the problem with modernist furniture—it looked great, but it wasn't meant to be comfortable.

After he took another long pull of bourbon, he forced himself to put the cap on it, even though he wasn't really that buzzed. He needed to keep his wits about him if he was going to tangle with the supernatural.

———•———

Sometime later he woke, blinking in the dimness at the unfamiliar space. He wasn't sure why he'd started awake, but his heart was pounding, and he remembered now where he was. Then he heard it: voices, whispering, just slightly louder than the background noise.

Listening intently, he sat up, but couldn't make out the words. There were definitely two voices, but not in conversation, rather talking over each other. He tried to directionalize it, stepping away from the sofa, but Jessica was right—it seemed like it was in the middle of the room. Turning slowly around, he focused on the sound, but then, abruptly, it stopped. He waited a minute, eyes closed, listening for more. Striding to the kitchen, squinting at the light, he flipped off the switch. The bedroom was quiet, and he waited there for a minute, standing in the dark at the end of the bed, but the voices seemed to be finished.

His phone said it was 3:36, and back at the

sofa, he sat down and cracked the pint, taking a long drink. Stretching out again, he listened for the voices, for anything above the ambient noise of the metropolis, smiling to himself as the delicious amber warmth seeped into his brain, pulling him back toward sleep. That hadn't been scary at all.

THREE

Not sure where he was at first when he woke up, he knew he was alone, and knew that it would come to him eventually. When it did, he sat up and looked at his phone, checking his tracking app for Conrad's location. On his way through the Cahuenga Pass, crawling along the freeway, the moron, probably headed to his stupid job. Slater got up and pulled open the drapes, wincing at the bright morning light.

After he'd washed up he took his coveralls out of his satchel and pulled them on over his clothes, dropping his wiring pliers and the screwdrivers he'd brought into the deep pockets. Slinging on the satchel, he grabbed the stepladder and went out into the hall, carrying it purposefully up to the fourth floor. At the top of the stairs he paused to open his satchel and flip on the frequency jammer, illuminating a brilliant blue LED. Until he switched it off again, no one in the immediate vicinity would be able to use Wi-Fi or the cell networks. It was an extreme measure, he knew, and completely illegal, but it was necessary to interrupt the camera mounted in the fourth-floor hallway, which was almost certainly broadcasting wirelessly.

The camera, small and black, with a clear plastic bubble over the lens, was right where Max had said it was, he saw, stepping into the hallway and pulling open the ladder below it. Glancing at the door to 402, he saw the high-security lock Max had photographed, and the camera lens where the peephole should be. He turned his back to the door and climbed toward the camera, digging in his satchel for the EMP generator, another blatantly illegal device he'd bought from the Russians, who supplied him with primo black-market surveillance gear.

The EMP generator looked like a photographer's bulb hood, a metal bell shape with the battery and workings mounted in a black box at the base. At close range the electromagnetic pulse it created would fry any and all unshielded electronics. The metal hood was necessary to protect anything not in its intended path—his phone in his pocket, nearby computers, radios and TVs. Aimed at the right spot, it could even disable a car.

Slater reached up and put the hood over the camera, holding the rim against the wall around it, and pressed the red button. It made a loud mechanical *snap* and then a high-pitched whine. The screwdriver he'd brought wasn't necessary, he found, as the camera was mounted with a sticky foam pad, and he easily pried it off the wall. As he'd suspected, there were no wires to be cut.

Stowing the EMP generator and the camera in his satchel, he took out the WET PAINT sign and peeled the backing off its adhesive strip, tacking it on the wall nearby.

No one had walked past, but he wasn't going to linger, in case the owner of the little camera noticed it had gone offline. Descending the ladder, he quickly folded it closed and headed down the stairs, scanning the hallways to make sure he was unobserved, and ducked back into 302. Propping the ladder against the wall by the door and setting his satchel on the end of the sofa, he pulled out his phone and texted Max:

I got the camera.

When he hit SEND, the phone informed him, "Message will be sent when phone is in range."

The jammer, he remembered. That was sloppy—he was jamming himself. Flipping open his satchel, he killed the device, extinguishing the blue LED, intentionally so bright as to be hard to overlook. Knocking out people's connectivity for more than a few minutes was a great way to attract unwanted attention.

Examining the camera, he could find no markings on it. It was heavy, probably containing a sizeable battery, and made of plastic, with no metal shielding, so the EMP blast had almost certainly fried its chips. Even so, he dug a black latex glove out of his satchel and stuffed the device inside, preventing the lens from seeing anything, on the off chance it had survived the death ray.

The question was, who had put it up there? Most likely it was the tenant in 402, but that wasn't a given. Hopefully the wet-paint sign would fool its owner into thinking a painter had pulled it down temporarily. It was a perfect ruse, in a way, as the only recourse was to ask the landlord who had taken it—but no one would want to admit to planting such a clearly illicit device in a shared space.

After he stripped off his coveralls, Slater went into the kitchen and looked in the fridge. Jessica and Mike had left a couple of tomatoes, the good kind that cost a fortune, not the basic mealy ones from a factory. They must have intended them for him and Max, he reasoned, eating them over the sink. No one would leave fresh food in the fridge when they were away for almost a week.

Even more compelling was a brick of vegan cheese in the fridge door. It was delicious, and he savored it, slicing off a couple of thin chunks, knowing how crazy expensive it was. Just as he put the knife in the dishwasher, there was a knock at the door.

Max, he saw, peering through the peephole, and opened it for him. Today he had on his gray grid-pattern suit. It was nice to see him wearing it, as Slater had helped pick it out. Max had been hesitant at first, claiming the fabric was too loud, but it looked good on him.

"What did you find?" Max asked, closing the door behind him.

Slater went to his satchel, lying on the end of the sofa, and handed Max the latex-gloved camera.

"Is it transmitting?" Max asked.

"I zapped it with the EMP generator, so it pretty much has to be dead. But just in case, don't look into the lens."

Max peeled back the glove, looking at the device. "I've never seen anything like this. I can't tell if it uses Wi-Fi or the cell network. Should we break it open?"

"I figured if you didn't recognize it, maybe I'll ask the Russians," Slater said.

"Good idea. It might even be theirs."

Slater pulled out his phone and texted Svetlana:

Can I drop by your office?

"So I heard the ghosts," Slater said, sliding his phone back into his jeans.

"Seriously?" Max said, frowning. "I half thought they might have been imagining it."

"I couldn't tell where it was coming from, but it was clear enough."

"Which room was it in?"

"I crashed on the sofa, and woke up around three thirty." Slater stepped over beside the coffee table. "Standing right here, it sounded like it was all around me. Just two voices whispering, but no babies, no running water. They stopped before I got into the bedroom."

"Why would a ghost use such a precise time slot? That alone is suspicious. Were you scared?"

Slater scoffed. "Jessica said it wasn't really scary, and that's the way it felt to me too—strange, but not supernatural."

"No surprise there," Max said. "Ghosts are bullshit."

Slater's phone buzzed in his pants, and he

pulled it out to check. It was Svetlana's response:

Here all day. Come any time.

"Looks like I'm going to Glendale," Slater said.

Max nodded. "I'll go talk to the building management. Do you want me to take the ladder? I was able to park fairly close."

"We might need it again," Slater said, and digging Mike and Jessica's keys out of his pocket, tossed them to Max, then pulled his satchel onto his shoulder. Max followed him out into the hall, locking the deadbolt.

It was a long walk back to the Thunderbird, but he was happy to find it unmolested, sleek and black and beautiful, and hot and sweaty inside from the morning sun until he got the air-conditioning blasting. In the daylight he realized he'd parked almost at Fairfax Avenue, and so he drove that way, stopping in at a deli that had a good bakery. Slater wouldn't eat any of this stuff, but his neighbor Grace, who didn't get out much, loved the rugelach.

Opening the trunk of his car, he stowed the pastries and pulled the heavy EMP generator and the jammer out of his satchel, taking the bag with him into the front seat. He knew the routine of visiting the Russians' workshop, and he needed to go in there light.

Glendale wasn't that far, but it was a slow trip, on surface streets all the way. Slater bought a lot of surveillance gear from Igor and his sister, Svetlana, and recently he'd been told to deal with her exclusively, as Igor was going away. It wasn't clear whether that meant he was being incarcerated or if he was fleeing the country, but maybe he was just traveling, because Svetlana was still in business. Their gear worked really well, and most of the devices interfaced with the smart-phone apps they provided, labeled in a befuddling mishmash of Roman and Cyrillic. The ambiguity was totally worth it, though—collectively the tech had saved him many hours of tailing vehicular and pedestrian targets, many long nights of watchful stakeouts.

Lots of Glendale had been spiffed up and rebuilt in the last few decades, but not all of it. Slater parked in front of a desolate storefront, with peeling paint and metal mesh over the windows, the sagging awning marked GLENDALE EASTERN IMPORTS. No one had been through that front door in years, by the look of it. Slater climbed out, pulling on his satchel, and walked around to the alley and the back door, steel-lined and unmarked, with a heavily armored lock. Pressing the bell, he heard a muted buzzer sound somewhere inside, and remembered to stoop a little to look into the camera. Before long the lock snapped open, and he pulled on the handle, stepping inside.

A ruddy guy in a dark suit was waiting in the anteroom, and gestured for Slater to raise his arms. This was the Russian equivalent of a guy like Max, the heavy. After a quick pat-down, he looked in Slater's satchel, pulling out the little bubble camera, still in its glove. He weighed it in his palm, and put it back.

Stepping to the inner door, the guy held his wrist against the sensor, and the lock clicked open. Inside was a long workroom, stools in front of benches piled with gutted electronics, plastic housing, and myriad tools, all bathed in harsh fluorescent light. The air had the tang of hot plastic and machine oil. Slater stepped toward the back and the room's lone occupant.

The guy in the suit left through another doorway, and Svetlana, perched on a stool, turned to greet him. She was in her fifties and a little heavy, her hair in a tight bun, and today she was clad in jeans and a fuchsia top. Always with the vibrant clothes and dramatic red lipstick, Slater wondered if she might be schizophrenic; choosing bright colors was a sign of that.

Slater greeted her with *"Dobroye utro."*

Svetlana broke into a smile and answered in Russian.

"I only know a few words," Slater said, shrugging.

"Still, you've been studying," she said, with her slight accent. "Good for you."

"Did that guy use an implant in his hand to unlock the door?"

"RFID tags," she said, nodding. "We all have them. It speeds things up. You want to get that kind of system?"

"Maybe someday," he said. "It's a great idea."

"So none of your subscriptions are due—I checked. You need something new?"

"I need help identifying a component." Slater pulled the gloved camera out of his satchel and handed it to her.

She pulled off the latex glove, examining the device. "Nothing I've seen before."

"It's wireless, right, but I think I disabled it. I blasted it with your EMP generator."

"In that case, I'm thinking you don't plan to return it to where it came from."

"I don't."

She turned back to the workbench, reaching for the wall rack and taking down a claw hammer, heavy and incongruous with the surrounding array of delicate electronics. It was something a construction worker would use, but she positioned the camera on its side and raised the hammer, dropping it onto the plastic housing with a loud *crack* and popping it open.

Watching her, Slater shifted his weight

from one foot to the other. She was a total pro, deftly cleaving that device like a jeweler cutting diamonds.

Putting on a pair of eyeglasses with a loupe attached to the left lens, Svetlana examined the chips on the newly exposed circuit board, then turned to her laptop and typed something, studying the screen over her glasses. Turning back to the device, she peered at it again.

"*Moosar,*" she said finally, turning back to Slater. "Chinese trash. It has a Wi-Fi chip in it, so even if you didn't manage to fry it, it's not connected to anything now."

So whoever was using it had to be near that hallway. "Why is it trash?" he asked.

"It's off the shelf, not custom-made, like my products. Based on the guts, it's probably worth about a hundred dollars."

"Can you tell who might have sold it?"

She shrugged. "It's a consumer product. Check online shopping."

The lock on the inner door snapped open, and a pasty blond guy came in, wearing baggy jeans and a heavy work shirt, despite the heat of the day. He eyed Slater as he closed the door behind him.

"Slater, this is Garik," Svetlana said. "He's working with me."

"Hey," Slater said, and Garik mumbled a

reply, dropping his gaze and sitting on a stool at the workbench, hunching over to focus on a little blue circuit board.

"You'd think he speaks no English," Svetlana said, looking sidelong at Garik. Then shooting Slater a sly grin, added, "You two actually have a lot in common."

"Is that so," Slater said, raising his eyebrows. Interesting that she would try to play match-maker. The guy was fuckable, but that would be risky. He didn't want to get on the wrong side of these people.

"Where did you find this camera?" Svetlana asked.

"Mounted in the hallway of an apartment building."

"Not the landlord, then. In your own building you'd hardwire the cameras. Someone was watching the neighbors."

Slater nodded. "I need to watch them back, but it has to be undetectable."

"Smoke detectors. People put those stupid things everywhere."

"I have a set of those that you sold me," Slater said, "but the battery only lasts for a day, and they're not wireless, so I have to go back and pull out the memory card."

"We call that the one-off model, good for a day or two. Short-term use only. Changing the smoke detector every day gets suspicious. You should go hardwired."

"Is that something you can help me with?"

"Absolutely. Take down the smoke detector that's already in that hallway. It will be there, I know it will, because those things are absolutely everywhere." Svetlana gestured broadly, scowling, as if it were a personal affront. "Garik here can put a camera in it that broadcasts over the cell network. It uses our standard software, phone app or Web browser. With AC power from the wall, you can watch that hallway until the sun burns out."

"Excellent," Slater said, grinning at her. "Can you do three of them?"

"As many as you need. The best thing is, it will still function as a smoke detector."

"I'll be back with them in a few hours."

"Garik will be here," she said, and winked.

Slater stepped toward the door, turning to say, *"Da svidania."*

Svetlana cackled and waved, and the door lock snapped open.

Walking back around to the street and his car, he thought about Garik. Svetlana was marketing him hard. Maybe she didn't know any other guys to introduce him to. How did she know Slater was gay, anyway? He'd fuck the guy, if that's what he wanted, but he hoped it wasn't more than that.

He wasn't going to take him out to dinner, or walk on the beach, or buy him jewelry, or whatever it was that people did on dates. It might be moot anyway, as Garik had turned red at the very sight of Slater; he might be way too shy even to get started.

Climbing into the Thunderbird, he started the engine to get the cool air going, then texted Max:

Where are you?

Max's reply came a moment later:

office

Slater had to grin. With those thick stubby fingers, not meant for a little phone keyboard, Max was brusque by necessity.

Setting the navigation on his phone to take him downtown, it took him on the 5 and the 10 freeways, which felt counterintuitive, but it worked, even though the 5 was sluggish, and he pulled into the lot across from his building less than half an hour later. Max called out a greeting as he came in, and Slater went into his office, dropping into the chair in front of his desk.

"Any luck with the management at the Camellia building?"

"Oh, yeah," Max said. "There's one occupant

in 402, a guy named Cash López. In 202 there's a woman, June Barker. She's also the only name on the lease."

"So no babies in either apartment."

"The property manager didn't think there was anyone undeclared living in either unit. I also got Social Security numbers from her for both of these knuckleheads."

Slater frowned. "How did you manage that?"

"Cecile is a thoroughly charming woman."

"You mean she thought you were charming."

Max laughed. "She let me look through the tenant files. I know that's a huge no-no, but when I lay my mack down, few can resist." He turned to his computer and twisted the screen so that Slater could see it too. With a few clicks he pulled up a photo of a form with CREDIT CHECK APPLICATION printed across the top. It was grainy but legible when he zoomed in on the handwriting.

"I never thought of you as a mack daddy," Slater said, "but here's the irrefutable proof."

"There's good info on this form—phone numbers, emails, past addresses."

"Did you run background checks on them?"

Max nodded. "June in 202 has some speeding tickets, but nothing else. Cash in 402 is clean. He's young, like twenty-four."

"How old is 202?"

"June is thirty-five, something like that. Your

cop boyfriend could probably get photos of them."

"He's not my boyfriend. Share those documents with me, will you?" Slater said. "Amazing work, buddy."

Max grinned appreciatively. "Did the Russians know about that camera?"

"Svetlana says it was a cheap commercial Wi-Fi unit."

"Wi-Fi has limited range. It has to be the guy in 402 who put it up there."

"Probably," Slater said. "I'm thinking we need to install our own cameras."

"Won't Cash notice that—especially since his is missing?"

"The Russians can put a camera into the smoke detector that's already there. I'm glad we left your ladder in Jessica and Mike's apartment. I'm going to swing by and pull it down, along with the ones on the second and third floors."

"That's some serious surveillance." Max furrowed his brow. "Why not just swap them out for new ones? Then you only have to go up the ladder once, and you're not leaving a hole in the roof while they're being doctored."

"Good idea. I still have to go look at them, though, if I'm going to buy a similar version."

"I'm sure I have a picture of it."

Slater raised his eyebrows. "You photographed the hallway smoke detector?"

"I took a zillion photos of the third-floor hall, the doorways, and the inside of 302."

"Max, you are so much smarter than you look. Show me," Slater said, sitting up and resting his elbows on the desk.

Max scoffed and turned to the screen, scrolling through his photos.

"You did take a lot," Slater said.

"You never know what'll be useful, right? Like this." He nodded to the screen. "The ceiling in the third-floor hallway."

Slater peered at the image. "It looks like a cheap-ass hardware-store smoke detector to me."

"I'm sure the ones on 2 and 4 will be the same."

"You're right—I'll just go buy new ones."

"It's not like cars, right, where they change the design every year," Max said. "You'll be able to get the exact same thing."

Slater rose. "Share that photo with me, will you?"

"Before you go," Max said, and pulled a pair of keys from his jacket pocket, tossing them to Slater. "I had a set of 302 keys made for you."

Slater snagged them out of the air. "Wherever she is, I bet Jessica's blood pressure just went up."

In his own office, Slater opened the safe and took some bills from the stash of company cash they kept inside. On the envelope he added the date and how much he'd taken to the list of other deposits and withdrawals. It wasn't an optimal accounting system, but they did a lot of work in cash. Locking the safe again, he checked his phone for Conrad's location. The dumbass was at his station, which meant he was at his desk—perfect.

Heading down to his car, Slater drove to Rampart, near his apartment, just a few minutes away. Pulling up near the entrance to the station, he dialed Conrad's cell.

"Are you parked out front?" Conrad asked.

"That depends. Are you at your station?"

"How is it that you only ever call me when you're already here?"

"I don't know," Slater said irritably, trying to think quickly. "You're usually here, and I live right nearby."

"Well, I'm busy."

"Switch off the porn, zip up your fly, and come outside. It won't take long."

Conrad hung up, and Slater climbed out of the car, wandering up the steps toward the building's front door. Conrad would come out, he knew he would.

The guy was right to be suspicious, but Slater did not want him to figure out that he could track him. Pulling out his phone, he typed a reminder to work-call Conrad once in a while when he wasn't here.

The front door flew open and Conrad appeared, eyes narrowing at the sight of Slater and waving him over to the accessibility ramp, where his colleagues on their way by would be less likely to notice them. Conrad was thick and dark and barrel-chested, even without his ballistic vest on, his black hair luxuriant despite his stupid cop haircut. Such a beautiful man.

"What do you want?" Conrad demanded, folding his arms.

"Why is it that you treat my mother like the most important person in the room," Slater said, "and you treat me like the guy you caught digging through your garbage cans?"

Conrad pointedly looked him up and down. "She dresses better, for one, and she doesn't regularly ask me to break the law."

"Why do you hang out with her, anyway?"

He sighed. "We don't hang out. I talk to her once in a while."

"Still, that's extremely suspicious."

"Is that why you called me out here? To tell me who I can and can't talk to?"

"Settle down," Slater said, furrowing his brow. "I need background on a couple of people for a case I'm working. Photos, specifically, and criminal records. As soon as you can."

Conrad glanced toward the door of the station, waiting as a tall woman in plainclothes stepped out, heading toward the sidewalk. "You're not the least bit concerned that I might get in trouble."

"It's your responsibility to be careful," Slater said, gesturing widely. "I can't hold your hand and walk you through it."

"You're also totally ungrateful. I help you a lot, you know."

"It's not like you have a choice, big guy. You know what happens if you don't play ball—I'll blow up your life."

"I help you because I choose to," he insisted. "Not because you threaten me."

Slater jutted out his chin. "You just do what you're told."

"I help you because you're a good guy, Slater. You know you are."

"So that's why you kicked me to the curb?" Slater demanded. "Because I'm a good guy?"

Conrad watched him for a moment. "You don't look hung over," he said finally. "Are you off the sauce?"

"Fuck you, Conrad."

"I'm asking because I'm concerned."

"You're asking because you're a total dick."

"And you're a sweet hot mess," Conrad said, with a sad smile. "Text me what you have on your targets."

"And make it snappy," Slater said, turning and walking back toward his car.

Conrad was gone by the time he climbed into the Thunderbird and looked back. Why did he have to be so abrasive? It was none of his business how much he drank, not anymore. *Because you're a good guy.* What did he know, the judgmental freaking idiot.

On his phone Slater found the forms Max had photographed, and texted the names and Social Security numbers to Conrad, then pushed thoughts of the guy out of his mind.

Pulling into the traffic, the streets were moving slow. There was a giant hardware store near here, he knew, but there was an even bigger one near the Russians in Glendale, and he headed that way.

It never ceased to amaze him how many people were out doing stuff in the middle of the day, jamming up the freeways, hogging up the parking at the hardware store. Once he got inside he stood in the smoke detector aisle, looking at the photos Max had shared with him on his phone. As he'd expected, he was able to find an exact match, and bought three of them.

Back at Glendale Eastern Imports, he parked out front and walked around to the alley. He waited a while after he'd rung, standing there with the hardware store bag dangling from his hand, and when the door finally unlocked, it was just Garik. There was no pat-down this time, and the lanky blond led him through to the workroom.

"You brought the smoke machines," Garik said, his accent thicker than Svetlana's.

"Smoke detectors," Slater said, handing him the bag. "Three of them."

Avoiding Slater's gaze, Garik sat at the workbench and pulled them out, deftly cutting through the thick plastic packaging on one with a wicked-looking utility knife. Once he had it out, Garik pried off the plastic cover to look at the innards.

Turning to Slater, he said gravely, "Sensors in these machines use radioactive material. The key is not to puncture the chamber with the isotopes inside. Gamma radiation is not good for you."

"That sounds wise," Slater said. "Let's try not to get irradiated."

Uninvited, Slater sat on the next stool, leaning back with his elbows on the bench, watching him work.

"Sveta says you like men," Garik said, not looking at him but picking up an electric drill and deftly changing the bit, then setting to work on the device's housing.

"I do," Slater said, raising his eyebrows. "Sveta means Svetlana?"

"It's a shorter name. Like Joe for Joseph."

"I don't remember ever telling her that I'm gay."

Garik shrugged. "She's intuitive."

"So what's your short name?" Slater asked, raising his voice over the sound of the drill.

"It's already shortened."

"What's your long name, then?"

Garik finally met his gaze. "You couldn't pronounce it."

"Fair enough." Slater watched him drill through the plastic housing.

Garik held it up, showing Slater the new hole. "Wide-angle lens in here, aiming down at forty-five degrees."

"Looks good," Slater said. "So do you ever go out and meet guys and other people?"

"Are you asking me to go out?"

"Maybe. I don't want to go on a date with you, and I don't need a boyfriend. But I'll sleep with you."

Garik looked down at the smoke detector, and tightly grasped Slater's shoulder with his hand. "I'd like that," he said, and let go.

Slater sighed. This was going to be weird. "Should I wait for these?"

"Go," Garik said. "I'll phone you. Probably it takes a few hours."

"Can I give you my number?"

"No need. We have it."

That sounded a little ominous, Slater thought, rising from the stool.

"But you can pay now," Garik said, looking up at him.

"Sure—how much?"

"Three hundred each. Includes app and Web access."

"How about a discount because they're all the same?"

"Very special price for you, because you're a loyal customer," Garik said. "Seven fifty."

Slater grinned. It sounded like Svetlana's words; they'd obviously discussed it in advance. Pulling out his wad of cash, he peeled off the appropriate C-notes and fifties, setting them on the workbench.

Garik frowned. "You're not going to negotiate some more?"

"Igor and Svetlana have been very good to me. The technology works every time, exactly the way they say it will. I wish everyone were so competent."

Walking to the door, he waited for the lock to click open before he walked out.

On his way back downtown, Slater was on the transition road to the 5 when his phone rang.

"Check your email," Conrad said when Slater answered. "I sent you DMV photos of your targets."

"Is there any dirt on these people?" Slater asked.

"The woman drives too fast and gets caught a lot."

"June."

"I think she works for a bunch of lawyers, because she contests every citation with a different attorney from the same firm downtown."

"Interesting," Slater said. "You put that together yourself? You should take the detectives exam."

Conrad scoffed at that. "The guy, Cash, got into trouble as a minor."

"For what?"

"Who knows? His juvie records are sealed."

"Come on, man, surely you can get into it." Gazing at the slowing sea of taillights stretching out ahead, Slater started to ride the brake pedal.

"I can't, not without ringing alarm bells somewhere."

"C-minus, then, on Cash," Slater said. "Solid A on June. Maybe E for 'effort' overall."

"I'll take that as a thank-you," Conrad said sharply. "You're welcome."

Slater hung up on him. Freaking idiot Conrad. He needed to accept the assessment and shut up about it.

Pulling into the lot by his office, he waved to the parking attendant, who was closing up for the day, and headed across the street. Upstairs he called a greeting to Max and sat at his own desk, opening his email to find the images Conrad had sent of June and Cash, both in the familiar washed-out tones and sky-blue background of a driver's license photo.

June was grinning slightly, eyes blank, looking above the camera. Cash was totally hot, wearing a glib expression. He looked young, with a great head of thick black hair and that indigenous look that people from some parts of Mexico had; maybe it was Mayan or Aztec. With a few mouse clicks he forwarded them to Max, then went into his office.

"So I got photos of the neighbors from Con-rad," he said, sitting in the chair in front of Max's desk. "They're in your email."

Max turned to his computer and pulled them up. "Downstairs June looks like a space cadet," he said.

"She works for lawyers, it seems."

"Lots of those people have entitlement issues," Max said, turning back to him. "There's a lawyer with the DA's office who lives in my build-ing. He parks his car in front of the elevators and takes the keys with him, like he's the only person who lives there. It drives the valets crazy."

Slater frowned. "You live in a building with valet parking?"

"Maybe June's trying to scare Mike and Jes-sica out so she can move into their apartment." He turned back to the screen and pulled up the photo of Cash.

"Dude has a criminal record from when he was a minor," Slater said, "but it's sealed."

"Seriously? Even a cop couldn't get into it?"

"He said it was too risky."

"So it could be anything—manslaughter, sex-ual assault."

"He's a brown kid," Slater said flatly. "It could be shoplifting a candy bar."

"A brown kid with a trendy name, so I'd say he grew up here." Max moved the photos side by side, gazing at them. "It would be great to see what these two are up to. What's happening with the smoke detector cameras?"

"I should get them today. I'll go over and put them up tonight."

"Working on a ladder after hours. I guess that's not too strange, if it's not too late."

"I'll wear my coveralls," Slater said, "and tell anyone who asks that it's an urgent repair type situation. I might sleep there again, unless you want to experience the ghost?"

"I can't tonight anyway."

"If June in 202 has an office job, how would you feel about letting ourselves in there during the workday? I know we can defeat her lock."

"Sure," Max said. "We might gain some insights."

"We'll do it after we get the cameras working, though, so we know when she leaves."

"There's another thing," Max said, looking down and taking a deep breath.

Slater's eyes narrowed. "What did you do?"

"Nothing," he said, bristling. "Not yet. I'm going out with Jessica's sister tonight."

"What's her name?"

"Vanessa. It's our third date. I wanted to ask you about that."

"What are you worried about? You managed to sweet-talk that apartment manager into committing a felony by opening her files."

"That's just about being charming," Max said. "It wears thin after you get to know me a little."

"Well, I can't really advise you. I've never been on a third date."

"Funny," Max said, even though Slater wasn't joking. "So what do I wear? I've had on two different suits with her. Should I wear one of those again, or a third one, or go in chinos?"

"It kind of depends on where you're going, don't you think?"

"A steak house, on Fig. It's upscale."

"Have you worn the black suit?"

"Not yet."

"There's your answer. You'll look sharp, and not overdressed in a place like that."

Max nodded. "That makes sense."

"Wear a dark-red tie. Why is the third date important?"

"I'm not sure how you guys do things, but for straight people the third date is the sex date. I need to be ready for that possibility."

Slater frowned. "That seems like a lot of groundwork. For me, the first date is the sex date. And it's not called the first date, because there's only ever one. It's not called a date either, unless I'm translating into hetero-speak."

Max held up his palms. "I get it, Slater. Thanks for your advice."

"Just be yourself. If she's up for a third date, she's already into you."

———•———

After a short night on an uncomfortable sofa, Slater needed to sleep. His dingy little apartment wasn't far from the office, in gritty Westlake, two flights up over a cell phone store. The best feature, the reason he'd chosen the place, was the secure private garage for his wheels.

It took a while to get there in the evening traffic, but eventually he pulled into the alley, waiting for his garage door to roll up. He took the pastries he'd bought this morning out of the trunk, enjoying their sweet aroma as he made sure the door rolled all the way closed. Pulling on his satchel, he trudged up the stairs, pausing at the door adjacent to his own, and knocked firmly.

Grace pulled it open, revealing her cloud of gray hair and watery eyes. She was in her eighties and lived alone, so Slater checked in on her once in a while. She'd helped him out before too; they had an understanding.

"You should look through your peephole before you open the door," he said.

She grinned. "I know your knock."

"I was over on Fairfax, so I brought you some rugelach."

"Oh, you know what I like," she said, reaching

for the bag. "Thank you, dear." Looking him over, she cocked her head. "You look tired."

"I'm not surprised—I had a late night."

"Well, take care of yourself," she said, and stepped back inside as Slater moved to unlock his own door.

The space was basically one big room that didn't get much light, with stained carpeting and an ancient bland beige paint job. A thrift-store sofa and a recliner sat beyond the kitchen counter, and off to one side was his bedroom. The one piece of furniture he'd bought new was his futon.

Stepping inside, he locked the deadbolt and admired the fifth of bourbon sitting on the counter, almost full. But he couldn't go there, not yet—the day wasn't over. Stripping off his clothes and leaving them on the bedroom floor, he went to take a shower and then padded back to bed, falling asleep as soon as he lay down.

———·———

His phone woke him, and scrabbling for it on the bedside table, he saw that it was Svetlana's number.

"Your smoke machines are ready," Garik said, when Slater answered.

"Excellent. Do you want to bring them by my apartment? We could get to know each other better."

"Do you have roommates?"

"No, man, I live alone. That's why I'm inviting you. One-on-one time."

"I see," Garik said, and after a long pause, "Yes, I will come."

Slater recited his address, then set his alarm for half an hour, sinking back into sleep.

When he woke, he collected the dirty clothes from the bedroom floor and dumped them in the closet, pulling on his jeans and a clean T-shirt. He moved the bourbon bottle into the cupboard and out of view, and soon there was a knock at the door.

When Slater pulled it open, Garik stepped in, setting a plastic bag on the kitchen counter.

"All you have to do is connect the power," he said, holding the bag open and showing him one of the devices. "I've already registered them to your account, so no need for any new software."

"Thanks," Slater said, and had to grin. The guy was talking like it was a legitimate business, clothing or housewares or insurance, not something completely underhanded.

"Nice apartment," Garik said, stepping past the kitchen counter and looking around.

"It's not, and I'm aware of that. Most people say, 'What a rat hole.'"

Garik turned to him, not meeting his gaze. "It's nice because you're in it."

Slater chuckled. "That's a very good attitude."

"I like your shirt," Garik said. "I mean, I like your chest in your shirt. You have a beautiful shape."

Slater stepped closer to him, taking his hands and placing them on his chest. His palms were warm, and he moved them over Slater's torso. Slater moved to kiss him, and Garik let him, his lips flaccid, not really kissing back. It was as if he had no muscle strength, or had never kissed anyone before. His mouth had an odd acidic taste, maybe from tobacco.

Leading him into the bedroom, Slater pulled off his own shirt, then Garik's, letting the guy run his hands over him again, then pulling him down onto the bed on top of him. Garik grinned and rolled to the side, and Slater groped his pants, feeling his swelling cock. But Garik was only receptive, taking no action, waiting for Slater to do the work.

Slater unbuttoned Garik's pants and slid them off, squeezing his cock, then stood up and peeled off his own jeans. "I'm going to fuck you," he said.

Garik nodded, and Slater found a condom in the bedside drawer, rolling it on his rock-hard cock, and then climbed on Garik, massaging a lubed finger inside him, then another, and finally penetrating him. As Slater got into it, Garik had a pained look on his face, his eyes screwed shut.

"Am I hurting you?" Slater asked, pausing.

"No—continue," he said, surprised, opening his eyes.

Slater ran his hands over Garik's chest, pounding him, ignoring his seeming discomfort, until he came. Pulling out, he took Garik's swollen cock into his mouth, and almost instantly Garik came too, grimacing and arching his back.

Slater lay down beside him, and after he'd caught his breath, asked, "How long have you worked for Svetlana and Igor?"

"Igor's away," Garik said.

"Where?"

"Overseas. I'm doing some of the work until he gets back."

"Are you related to them?" Slater asked, eyeing him.

"You mean like family? Sveta is my aunt, but not through blood. Do you call that an aunt? She's a good friend of my parents."

"Sounds like an aunt to me."

"May I shower?"

"Go for it," Slater said, relieved that he might not be planning to stay for long.

Slater lay there, watching the fading daylight in the grimy window, listening to him turn on the water, not a word of complaint about the grungy bathtub. Maybe he lived somewhere worse.

When he came back, Garik pulled his pants on and looked around for his shirt. Grateful that he didn't have to throw him out, Slater got up and got dressed as well. He hated having obligations to other people, and Garik was just that—a relative of someone he couldn't afford to alienate.

After Garik left, he ate some peanut butter out of the jar with a spoon, and found a vegan Pop-Tart in a ripped-open box in the cupboard, eating it over the sink. After he loaded the smoke detectors into his satchel, he locked up the apartment and trotted down to his garage, heading west to the Miracle Mile.

Even though it was completely dark by the time he arrived, in a stroke of luck he found a parking spot on the same block as the Camellia building, under one of the young bauhinias, just a couple of minutes' walk to the lush courtyard entryway. Inside 302, he pulled on his blue coveralls, put his wiring pliers and a couple of screwdrivers into the pockets, and took the ladder and one of the devices into the hall.

Looking around to make sure he was unobserved, he set up the ladder and climbed it, twisting the smoke detector, gingerly pulling it down to expose the wiring. It was a little dangerous to work with hot wires, but Garik had thoughtfully included yellow twist-on wire connectors, and the mount for the unit was the same as the one already attached to the ceiling. Once he'd carefully disconnected the wires and attached them to the new device, it snapped easily into the mount with a satisfying *click*. Garik had engineered it so that it rotated, and he twisted it until the discreet opening he'd drilled in it for the camera lens was pointing toward Mike and Jessica's dark-orange front door.

Stepping inside to grab another doctored device, he carried the ladder downstairs, climbing up and repeating the procedure with the smoke detector on the second floor. As he was working, a woman in a gray suit walked up the stairs and approached the ladder. Her face was familiar— June, the tenant in 202. She glanced at him but stepped past the ladder, rattling her keys at her front door.

With his dark Latin features, and wearing coveralls, tools in hand, Slater fit the profile of most of the city's manual laborers, so doing stuff like this rarely got him a second look from anyone. But June paused, gazing up at him.

"What's the trouble up there?" she asked.

"Just changing the batteries," Slater said, affecting a Spanish accent.

"It looks like you're swapping out the whole thing."

"*Jess*," Slater said. "This one has some problems."

"Can I have the broken one?"

"Why? Don't you have one inside your apartment?"

"It's just that it looks kind of cool," she said.

"I can't give it to you. When it's broken it can leak gamma radiation. You don't want that in your apartment."

June scoffed, and went back to her door, stepping inside. Slater heard the deadbolt slide closed.

Up on the fourth floor, Slater worked quickly, keeping his back to the door of 402. Moving the ladder under the wet paint sign, he pulled it down, then carried everything down the stairs, glancing around to make sure he was alone before stepping into Jessica and Mike's apartment.

Leaning the ladder on the wall beside the door, he peeled off his coveralls, feeling sweaty in them even though it was cooler in the building than it was outside, tossing them on the Barcelona chair. Standing there cooling off, his eye followed the curving staircase, laden with books and photos, up to the blank ceiling. On the ceiling here they'd put up drywall to separate the apartments, but what did it look like in 402?

He pulled out his phone and sank onto the sofa, starting one of the Russian apps. Its inscrutable label read "камеры," but the icon was self-explanatory, an old motion-picture camera with black housing for spools of film. Garik was true to his word, and all three cameras were already operating and online, aimed at each of the doorways, the image in beautiful full color. It took a minute of fiddling with the options, but eventually he managed to set the software to record video whenever there was motion in the frame.

Kicking his boots off, he got up to find the unopened pint of bourbon he'd stuffed in his satchel, then killed the lights and stretched out on the sofa, taking a long pull from the bottle and coughing as it overwhelmed him, burning the back of his nostrils. It was so worth it, the golden burn in his throat, warming his gut, and he relished the feeling of his muscles and his mind starting to unspool.

———◆———

A baby crying, he thought, waking in darkness. Where was he that had a baby? Then he remembered, and sat up, listening. It was soft, but clearly audible, and when he got to his feet, it sounded louder. It faded as he walked down the hall to the bedroom, but standing there at the end of Mike and Jessica's bed, it was louder again.

Stepping toward the walls, the sobbing didn't seem to shift position, but he stopped short when a voice spoke over the sound of the baby.

"Leave …" it whispered. "Leave this place …"

Slater closed his eyes, concentrating on the voice. It repeated the words a minute later, and eventually the baby faded out, and there was only the background hum of the metropolis. A car rolled by on Sixth Street, the hiss of tires on asphalt breaking the spell.

Back at the sofa, he checked his phone. It was 3:42, meaning it must have started around the same time again. Max was right—it felt too consistent. It was hard to believe that a supernatural entity would be punching a clock.

Stretching out again, Slater took a deep drink from the pint, and listened to the quiet apartment, eventually drifting off.

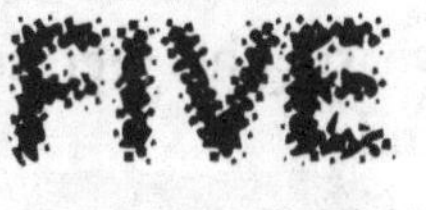

FIVE

aking and opening the drapes, Slater winced at the bright daylight. It looked hot out. After he washed up he scanned the fridge, dipping a spoon into the jar of high-end almond butter, eating a couple of pickles, some OJ, an apple. It was crisp and thoroughly flavorful, nearly an archetypally perfect apple—these people must buy their food at spendy places.

Sitting at the dining table, he checked his phone for Conrad, at his station already, the idiot. The camera app had no hits from the third or fourth floor, but a few minutes ago, June had left her apartment, pausing to lock the deadbolt, dressed in a somber gray suit, her hair up. That looked like the kind of drag you'd wear to a law office. He texted Max:

June left for work. Bring the key kit—and coveralls.

After he pulled on his jeans and his shirt, he stretched out on the sofa again, enjoying the sun streaming in the east windows, stirring again when there was a knock at the door. Max let himself in, todapy wearing his seersucker suit, a small duffel bag in hand.

"It's a lot easier to park around here during business hours," Max said, setting the bag on the floor.

Slater stood up and stretched his back. "How was the dreaded third date?"

"Pretty damn great. There was no sex, but that just means she's serious about me."

"Such an optimist," Slater said, running a hand through his hair. "I'd be frustrated with all the wasted time."

"Maybe I'll value it more when it does happen because it's not happening instantly."

Slater scoffed and went to pick up his coveralls where he'd left them, draped on the Barcelona chair. As he stepped into them, Max pulled his own pair out of his duffel bag, the same dark blue as Slater's so that they'd more easily pass for a work crew. Next he took out the key set, another shady tool from the Russians—a heavy binder filled with dozens of pages of hardware-store master keys, each in a numbered pouch. The genius part of it was the key-shaped probe that connected to a cell phone and read the lock, spewing out the number for the correct key. It didn't work with exotic locks, but most people didn't have those.

"I'll run down and see what we get," Slater said, gesturing for the probe, which he plugged into his phone. He didn't even have to start the key app, as it launched itself—that was new. The screen went black, displaying the word "готов."

No one was in the hallway, and he trotted down the stairs, scanning the second floor to make sure he was unobserved before he stepped up to the door to 202 and stood close, slipping the probe into the lock. The screen went red, unable to get a reading, and he adjusted the probe slightly. Almost instantly the app went green and read "421"—that was all he needed to know.

Back in Mike and Jessica's apartment, Max was pulling on his coveralls. "Got it?" he asked.

"Hooray for corporate hegemony and the limited range of lock manufacturers. It came up with just the one possibility," Slater said, stooping at the key case and flipping heavy pages to find the key marked 421.

Max was pulling on a dark ball cap. "Hooray for the Russians too. I checked the camera app this morning, and I've got access to all three cameras."

"Before we go down, maybe we should check again in case June came back."

Max pulled out his phone and tapped at it. "No activity since she left," he said finally, "except you sneaking around just now. She looked to me like she was dressed for the office."

Slater pulled on his satchel. "Let's go."

"What's the story if we're challenged?"

"We're plumbers, responding to a report of a leak on the ground floor."

"We don't have any tools," Max said. "It feels risky because I know the manager. It's why I brought the hat."

"Our tools are in the truck. If you see her, head the other way, and I'll deal with it."

Max nodded assent and went to the door, checking the peephole before he stepped out. When they got to the second floor, Slater reached into his satchel and flipped on the jammer, illuminating it's brilliant blue indicator.

At the door to 202, Slater knocked loudly and called, "Maintenance."

They stood, listening, but there was no response, no sound of movement inside. Slater unlocked the door with the master key, grinning as it twisted freely, easily sliding back the deadbolt. *Thank you, Svetlana.*

"Hello?" he called, pushing the door open, and Max quickly followed him in, closing it behind them and flicking on the lights.

"No alarm panel," Max said quietly. "Not surprising in a rental."

"Yikes—look at this place," Slater said.

It had the same layout as Mike and Jessica's apartment upstairs, but it was full of junk: cardboard boxes and books stacked on the floor, piles of clothes, and beneath it all, way too much furniture, jammed tightly and chockablock along the walls. One table had chairs stacked on it, and on top of those were more bags and boxes. With the windows half blocked and only narrow pathways between the mountains of junk, it looked much smaller than 302.

"What a mess," Max said, taking it in. "Look at all the garbage bags." Black plastic gardening-size bags were perched on tables and integrated into piles of clothes, but there were paper grocery bags and myriad other containers too.

"It's not actually garbage, though," Slater said. "It doesn't smell."

Walking back to the bedroom, Slater stepped inside. The degree of clutter was the same, with only a third of the bed accessible, the rest piled with clothes. More black leaf bags and clothes were piled waist-high in front of the closet.

At the end of the hall, the bathroom looked like the stockroom at a drugstore after an earthquake, a jumble of bottles and tubes and towels everywhere. At least the tub looked like it was still functioning.

Max was in the kitchen when Slater came back.

"I am not looking in that fridge," he said.

"Do you think someone this disorganized could be running a con on her neighbors?" Slater asked.

"I'm surprised she's even able to hold down a job."

"Nothing suspicious?"

"It's hard to look at everything," Max said, "but I didn't find any cameras." He pulled out his phone. "The jammer's been on for two minutes."

"We can go," Slater said, and checked the peephole.

Seeing no one, he stepped out into the hall and locked the door, and when they reached the stairs, flipped open his satchel and switched off the jammer.

Max was in front, and he paused on the stairs when a wild-haired man in boxer shorts and a T-shirt appeared at the top. The guy stopped when he saw them.

"Were you guys messing with the Internet?" he demanded.

"We do the plumbing," Slater said, using his thick fake Spanish accent and spreading his palms to demonstrate his innocence. His satchel probably didn't look like a plumber's gear, but their matching blue coveralls did.

"Is someone else working on the cable? I got kicked off."

"It's probably just a temporary glitch," Max said. "You know how the cable company is. Go try again."

The guy scowled at them but turned and headed back up.

Watching him go, they waited in the hallway until they heard a door close somewhere in the other wing, then headed back into 302.

"So the jammer definitely works," Max said, pulling off his cap.

Slater unzipped his coveralls. "I'm thinking this isn't about June."

Max nodded. "I get that feeling too."

"We need to focus on 402."

In his pocket, his phone buzzed, and at the same time Max's chimed. Max pulled out his phone and checked it.

"Speaking of 402," he said.

"Cash?" Slater said, and stepped over to look at Max's phone.

As they watched, Cash locked the door to 402, tucked the key into his pants pocket, and walked out of frame.

"That just happened?" Slater demanded.

"Less than a minute, by the time stamp."

"I'm going to follow him, but I've got all my stuff ..."

"I'll bring it to the office later," Max said quickly. "Go."

Not bothering to check the peephole, Slater went out into the hallway and down the stairs. There was no sign of Cash until he got out through the courtyard to the street. Half a block away, walking toward Wilshire, he caught sight of the red-and-yellow plaid shirt he'd just seen in the video on Max's phone. Striding rapidly to catch up, Slater passed the Thunderbird, and briefly considered climbing in and following him that way. He'd be able to keep up if Cash got into one of the vehicles on the block, but if he walked much farther, he'd lose him—no way could he follow a pedestrian in a car, at least not stealthily.

Slater kept walking, getting closer as Cash waited to cross the boulevard. The light turned, and Slater jogged to make it, now just a few yards behind Cash. There were lots of pedestrians here, so the fact that he was tailing him wasn't obvious, and he let a couple of people get between them. The guy wasn't wasting any time, walking purposefully and not looking into the eclectic array of shops that lined this stretch of Wilshire. At the end of the block, in front of the post office, he stopped, looking at the traffic with half a dozen other people who were standing there waiting. The express bus stop, Slater realized. Interesting that a guy with an eight-hundred-dollar lock on his door was taking the bus—although admittedly the express lines were the only routes frequented by middle-class Angelenos.

Slater stood back by the wall of the post office, watching Cash at the curb. The bus pulled in, and Cash boarded in the middle of the clot of other commuters. Slater kept a transit card in his wallet, and fished it out now, boarding after everyone else. It wasn't that crowded, and Slater walked past Cash, who was staring blankly out the window, and sat a few rows back, behind the rear door but where he could keep an eye on the guy.

More people boarded than got off at every stop, and it felt like a long slog, all the way downtown, before Cash finally got up and disembarked, along with a large number of other passengers. Slater followed, stepping off among the crowd. They were in the Financial District, within walking distance of Slater's office.

Tailing the guy was even easier here on the crowded sidewalks, and Slater easily kept up as Cash made his way to Seventh Street and then ducked into a bank. Stopping at the ATM outside, he looked in. Cash was waiting in line for a teller, his back to the door. There was no other way out, so Slater abandoned the pretense of using the machine and loitered a few yards from the entrance.

It was a chain bank, so he could have gone to a branch in the Miracle Mile—unless he had a safe deposit box down here, or maybe a private banker. But Cash appeared soon after. It hadn't been long enough for him to have gone into the vault, or to have sat down with one of the suits. He headed east, and Slater tailed him until he turned into a doorway and disappeared. As he came up to it, Slater glanced inside. It was the narrow lobby of an office building, with a long list of tenants posted at the entrance. Cash was nowhere to be seen.

Rather than tailing him inside, Slater looked around for a vantage point to watch for him leaving again. There was a coffee place almost directly opposite, and Slater trotted across the street in a break in the traffic, sitting at an open table on the sidewalk. Pulling out his phone, he glanced at it, and kept it in his hand, but mostly looked past it, watching the lobby where his quarry had disappeared.

After twenty minutes he started to wonder if Cash had gone out another way. Even if he eventually returned, was there any point in watching him run errands? It hadn't been very enlightening so far, and Slater felt naked without his car, felt stranded being so far from it. Conrad was still at work, the dumbass, when he checked, and the camera app showed no new movement in the halls since Cash had left, and slightly afterward on the third floor when Slater had left. Maybe he should get on the bus and go back there to rescue his wheels.

But then Cash came out of the lobby and went east. Slater jumped up and followed, on the other side of the street, until Cash turned on Broadway. Hustling to catch up, he caught sight of the plaid shirt climbing an exterior staircase. Slater had to grin—he knew this place, a cruisy guy's pub. Cash was in Slater's world now.

About to mount the stairs, he paused when his phone buzzed in his pocket, and pulled it out to check. It was a text from Max:

Just saw Cash leave the apartment.

Frowning, Slater typed a quick reply:

I've got eyes on him, and I'm downtown.

Max's response came before he got halfway up the stairs:

I'm sure it's the same guy. I'm following him.

Had Slater tailed the wrong man? Thinking about it, he'd been following that distinctive plaid shirt and the coiffed black hair, but had he gotten a good look at his face?

Walking in, Slater scanned the pub. He'd never been here before dark, and it looked different, brightly lit by the big windows. During the daytime it clearly wasn't just about drinking, as the people sitting at the tables had plates of food. Cash was perched on a barstool near the register, so Slater headed there, sitting two stools away. As he sat down, Cash glanced up from his phone screen, acknowledging him with a grin. This was definitely the guy from the DMV photo, no ambiguity—Max must have it wrong.

The guy didn't have a drink in front of him, so Slater leaned toward him. "Can I buy you a beer?"

"No—but thanks," he said.

At least he'd smiled, Slater thought, and ordered a Corona when the bartender came by, dropping a sawbuck on the counter. It was usually easier than this to pick up guys. When someone said "no," there were always lots of others to move on to, and he never got stuck on just the one. But he was going to have to be polite and witty and chatty to connect with this guy, sitting here sober and in broad daylight. It seemed like an overwhelming task. Maybe this wasn't Slater's world after all.

But Cash saved him the effort. "You look Latin American," he said, setting his phone down, "but you don't sound it."

Slater responded amiably, even though a

comment like that usually made him want to punch the guy in the face. "My father was Salvadoran. I don't really have a connection to the culture, though, and sadly I don't speak Spanish."

"It's the same for me," Cash said. "Too many generations here to keep the language, even in a city like this."

The bartender set down Slater's Corona and whisked away the ten.

"I guess we're non-Hispanic Hispanics," Slater said.

Cash laughed. "Do you come here for lunch?"

"Sometimes," Slater lied.

"The food is pretty good, and there's always lots of guys."

"That's why I'm here," Slater said, eyeing him intently.

Cash blushed but held his gaze, but then looked away when someone behind the bar called, "Logan?"

"That's me," Cash said, and stood up. A woman in a black T-shirt, her hair bundled up and looking hot and sweaty, handed him a white bag with a couple of take-out trays inside, the plastic knotted at the top.

"Before you go," Slater said, "Can I get your number?"

Cash hesitated, but said, "How about you give me yours?" Pulling out his phone, he held it awkwardly, swiping at it with one thumb, the food bag swaying in his other hand.

"I'll input it for you," Slater said, and waved for the phone.

When Cash handed it to him, he quickly opened the messaging app, typed "Slater" and his number, and texted himself. In his pants he felt his own phone buzz.

"I'm not sure what I did," Slater said, frowning and handing it back. "I think it's in there, and I put my name."

"What is your name?" Cash asked, eyeing him and pocketing the phone.

"Slater."

He nodded. "I'm Cash. Bye, Slater."

If he copped to being Cash, why had the staffer called him Logan? It wasn't his surname. Taking a pull of his beer, Slater watched him head toward the stairs. That was the end of it—now that they'd met, he couldn't safely tail him anymore.

Waving the bartender over, Slater asked, "What can you do that's vegan?"

The guy frowned thoughtfully. "Maybe tortilla chips. Is salsa vegan?"

"No thanks," Slater said, and drained his beer, then scooped up some of his change and headed for the stairs.

The office wasn't far, but it was the hottest part of the day, and he worked up a sweat walking over. When he got upstairs the lights were off, their three little rooms quiet, and even inside, once the front door was closed, he could hear the sewing machines in the neighboring factories cycling on and off.

Sitting at his desk with his feet up, gradually cooling off, he made some notes on his computer. Cash's phone number was the same as the one he'd used on the apartment credit-check application, but he couldn't find anything more when he searched for it online. The guy was suspiciously absent from social media too, with no accounts that Slater could see, not even passing mentions by other people.

Slater picked up his phone again and dialed Andy's number. It took him a minute to answer, with his familiar distorted intonation, but when he did his words made Slater smile.

"It's the denim-clad pugilist."

"I've got a job for you," Slater said. "I have a phone number and an email address for a guy, and I want you to break into them."

"I can't do that," Andy said. "I'm not a hacker."

"Well, maybe you can find something about this guy that I can't, without actually hacking him. Like I said, it's about information."

"I guess I could … look into it."

"Can I read you the info?"

"I'm not your damn secretary," Andy said, "and I don't take dictation. Text it to me."

Slater chuckled. "What's this going to cost me?"

"That's easy—sex."

"At least I know I can afford it. Call me when you have something," Slater said, and ended the call.

That was completely stupid, trading sex for work, when sex was as free as the air. Maybe it was harder for Andy to get it, though, with his limited mobility. Still, with a hookup app, he could make guys come to him, and there were always tons of them around.

Keys rattled in the front door, and Max pushed

his way in, laden with his duffel bag and Slater's satchel, the blue cuff of his coveralls hanging out at one side. Slater swung his feet down as Max set the bag on the desk and sank into the chair.

"That stuff is heavy," Max said, sweat glistening on his brow. "So who were you actually tailing?"

"The guy in the DMV photo, I'm sure of it. I sat beside him in a bar and got his phone number."

"For a date?"

"He's one of my people," Slater said. "His phone number matches the one on the credit-check application you photographed."

Max frowned. "Watch the hallway video and tell me it's not the same guy."

Slater found the camera archive on the Web. First he clicked on the earlier video, time-stamped when Slater had gone after him, and repositioned the monitor so Max could see it.

"This is the guy I tailed," Slater said. "He was wearing that shirt. We took the bus downtown and dicked around for a while, and then he bought lunch in a bar. I sat down and flirted with him."

"Watch the other video," Max said, gesturing to the screen.

It was time-stamped an hour later. Cash stepped out of the door marked 402, wearing the red and yellow plaid shirt, then locked it and walked out of view.

"It's a software glitch," Slater said. "It's the same clip."

"It's not—I checked. The second one takes longer to lock the door, and then he adjusts his hair with his hand. The first guy didn't do that."

"So it happened earlier in the day and it's mislabeled."

Max slapped the desktop. "When this video came up, I followed him out to the street. I was tailing the guy in the video. He climbed onto a motorcycle and put on a helmet, but he was wearing that same damn shirt. I texted you right as I was leaving 302."

Slater frowned. "Where did he go?"

"I got in my car and tailed him for a few blocks, but he was lane-splitting, and I couldn't keep up. Last time I saw him, he was heading west on Sixth."

Slater stared at him. "Twins?"

"I can't think of any other logical explanation, unless he's a time-traveler. But there was only one name on the lease."

"Maybe only one of them lives there. But why would two grown men be dressed exactly the same?"

Max shrugged. "I knew a pair of twins in high school who did that to get with more girls.

One of them would get friendly, and then both of them could go out with her. It was half the work."

"Maybe that's it—they're posing as one person, so there's one name on the lease. Mine took the bus, so maybe they're sharing that motorcycle. At the bar he told me his name was Cash, but he used a different name for the food order—the server called him Logan."

"I never use my real name in a coffee place."

"Still," Slater said, "even if they want people to think there's only one of them, they're not going to have the same name."

"It seems odd, but it still makes more sense than a software glitch."

"The truth isn't always simple, but it's always elegant," Slater said. "That has to be it: there are two of them."

Max rose. "I'm glad we're not seeing double, at least. Maybe I'll sleep over there tonight, and see if I can hear the ghosts. Do you need a ride back to your car?"

"I'll pick it up later," Slater said. "I need to sleep."

Max went to his own office, and Slater took a minute to plug in the jammer to recharge and to stow the EMP generator in the safe, then called good-bye to Max. Down on the sidewalk again it was hot, but the metro was just a few blocks' walk. It felt strange to be carless, like he was too exposed, more vulnerable to the chaos of the streets.

It was just two stops to his neighborhood, and soon he was climbing up out of the ground again, then walking up his own block. A package delivery truck was parked in front of the cell phone store under his apartment, and he ogled the driver, who was wearing a snug uniform, a shirt and short pants that matched the color of the truck, as he loaded boxes into it. The guy was a little thick and had nice legs, dark hair.

When he noticed Slater was checking him out, he said something in Spanish.

"Excuse me?" Slater said, pausing on the sidewalk.

"Have you got something for me?" he asked.

Slater put his hands on his hips. "That is such a loaded question."

"I just figured you were looking at the truck," he said, slamming the back door.

"That's not what I was looking at. You're in great shape."

The guy laughed. "I'm not, but I guess I have a little definition in my arms because of this job."

"When are you finished your shift?"

"Right now."

"I live upstairs," Slater said, nodding toward the building. "You could come up and show me the rest."

The guy's eyes grew wide. "Man, I love this town."

"Is that a yes?"

"I should probably move my truck first. This is a loading zone."

"You'll never find another parking spot," Slater said. "Tell you what—if you get cited, I'll pay for it." Even if Slater had to shell out, it would be worth it to discourage the guy from lingering.

He looked up the street, considering that. "I guess it's unlikely they'll enforce it so late in the day."

Slater waved for him to follow, and led him into the doorway beside the cell store.

"You're not crazy, are you?" the guy asked, following him up the stairs.

"It's hard to be objective about that. What's your name?"

"Matías."

Once they were in Slater's apartment, he locked the deadbolt, and Matías wandered past the kitchen into the main room.

"Wow—this is bleak."

"Thank you," Slater said, and moved closer. "So what are you into, Matías?"

Stepping up to him, Matías squeezed Slater's biceps, then ran a hand through his hair. "Flirting with strange men in the street—I think I should teach you some manners."

"You can try."

"Not painfully, though."

Slater looked him over. The guy was built thick, but Slater could still kick his ass if he needed to.

"Firm but not violent," Slater said. "I can do that." He put a hand on his cheek and leaned in to kiss him. The guy was good at it, his mouth welcoming, and strong, and responsive.

"Is that your bedroom?" Matías said. "Let's go."

"Make me."

Matías looked surprised, but then figured it out. Scowling, he grabbed Slater's wrist and twisted it behind his back, then frog-marched him into the bedroom. Matías pushed him onto the futon and then climbed up, straddling him.

"Can I slap you around?" Matías asked.

"I think we both know that's the only way I'm going to learn."

He struck Slater open-handed, tentatively and without much strength, on the cheek.

"You're going to have to do better than that," Slater said, slapping him back with the same wan force.

Matías frowned in concentration and slapped him harder, enough to twist Slater's head.

"Now I'm paying attention," Slater said.

He unbuttoned Slater's shirt and pulled off his boots and his jeans, then took off his own uniform shirt. Running his hands over Slater's body, he spent time exploring it, groping and kissing him, seemingly forgetting about being in charge.

"Are you going to fuck me?" Slater said finally, and pulled open his bedside drawer.

Matías dug out a condom, rolling it on his impressively hard cock, then roughly rolled Slater over, massaging a lubed digit inside him, then climbed up and penetrated him, pounding and grunting. Finally he came, roaring, and slid down, pinning Slater's arms behind him and grabbing his cock, stroking him intently until he came too.

It was kind of great to just roll with it, Slater thought, to be liberated from the work, unlike with Garik, where he had to do everything. Matías released his grip and moved in beside him, wrapping an arm around Slater's chest. As soon as he closed his eyes, Slater drifted into sleep.

———◆———

Later, Matías woke him as he shifted position. "I should go," he said. "I'm worried about my truck."

Slater sat up and rubbed his eyes. "How hard is it to replace your uniform?"

Matías frowned. "Why?"

"I want to buy it from you."

"Why do you need a delivery uniform?"

"I serve subpoenas for a living. A uniform like

that would make it easier."

"I get it," Matías said, nodding. "People always open the door for a package delivery."

"Will you sell it to me?"

He sighed. "Man, it just seems so sketchy. Won't it be too big for you?"

"It doesn't matter," Slater said. "Your name isn't on it, right, so it can never be traced to you, no matter what I do with it. I'll give you two hundred bucks."

His eyebrows shot up. "It's yours. I'll need some other clothes to go home in, though."

Slater got up and dug through the closet, finding a baggy T-shirt and tossing it to him, then looking for a pair of old sweatpants.

"Maybe I should try that," Matías said. "Serve subpoenas while I'm on my route."

"It's not that lucrative. Look at where I'm living."

"Yeah, I see that. How did you get into it?"

"Look online in the county court system. Read up on process servers, and you'll know whether you want to do it or not." Hopefully that sounded logical, he thought, not wanting to get further bogged down in the lie. It didn't really matter, though—the sex part was over, and the guy had already committed to selling his clothes.

Tossing him the sweatpants, Slater picked up his jeans and found two C-notes, handing them to Matías. The sweats fit him, it seemed, and he tied the cord at his waist, then cleaned out the pockets of his shorts.

"I'm keeping my belt," he said, coiling it up and then pulling on his shoes.

Slater went into the living room and stood at the window, peering down at the street below. "No ticket on your vehicle."

"Excellent," Matías said, and Slater followed him to the front door.

In the bedroom his phone rang: *No wire hangers! What's wire hangers doing in this closet, when I told you no wire hangers, ever?*

"Fuck," Slater muttered.

"Problem?" Matías said, twisting the deadbolt open.

"Just someone I don't want to deal with right now." Slater closed the door behind him and went into the bedroom for his phone.

"What do you need, Doris?" he demanded, answering the call.

"To talk to my son," she said. "Albert and I are going to an art opening downtown this evening. We wondered if you'd join us for dinner."

Slater heaved an audible sigh. No way was he going to sit down with his mother's putz boyfriend, even for an hour. "I can't make dinner, but I'll come with you to the opening."

They planned when to meet, and Slater

ended the call. Retrieving his car was going to have to wait.

In the bathroom he looked over his haggard face, dark circles under his eyes from lack of sleep. Like it or not, if he was going to see Doris, he had to shave.

Afterward he set his alarm and climbed back into bed.

SEVEN

aking up groggy, he ate the last granola bar in the kitchen cupboard and then put on a clean shirt, deciding the jeans were still passable. The walk to the metro station helped him wake up, despite the fading daylight, the shadows growing longer.

Standing at a pole on the train, his phone buzzed in his pants, and he pulled it out to check. The camera app had a new recording from the hallway outside 402, and he clicked on it to watch. Cash or his doppelgänger stepped into the frame, wearing the same plaid shirt, a grocery bag in hand, and dug his keys out of his pocket. As he pushed his way inside, Slater could hear the faint beeping of an alarm system, flat and tinny through his phone's speaker. The video ended when Cash shut the door behind him. If they had installed an alarm in a rental unit, there was definitely something hinky going on.

Stepping off the train, he trotted up the stairs to the street amid the sea of commuters. Near the station he stopped at a food truck that was parked at the curb and bought a couple of avocado tacos, eating them over the gutter before walking to Spring Street.

The smokers were gathered on the sidewalk in front of the gallery as he approached, making its location unmistakable. Narrow planter boxes crowded with horsetail fronted the venue on either side of the entrance. Why did people plant those? They were so piggy with the water, but perhaps the intention was to create a sleek and minimalist Asian vibe, as it looked a little like miniature bamboo. A fescue would have been a better choice—equally eye-catching, and local, at least, so you could ignore it, and save all that water. But nobody had asked Slater.

The gallery was already crowded when he stepped inside, and he caught sight of Doris toward the back of the space. A woman sitting at a table inside the door stopped him.

"You'll need a sticker for later," she said.

"I won't be here long."

"Everyone needs a sticker," she said firmly.

Slater sighed impatiently. "Fine."

The woman cocked her head, gazing up at him. "I wonder if you're an oak leaf, a wishbone, or a pepperoni slice?" Sheets with multiple copies of the three options were arrayed in front of her. Finally she looked back to the table and peeled off a wishbone sticker.

Slater glared at her. "Oak leaf," he said intently.

She frowned. "I'm thinking wishbone."

"Oak leaf," he repeated, raising his voice.

Concern in her eyes, she acquiesced, peeling off an oak leaf and rising to stick it on the left side of his chest.

Slater stopped at the bar, absently touching the glossy-feeling sticker on his shirt as he waited in line.

"Red or white?" the guy asked when it was his turn.

"Red," Slater said, and the guy handed him a plastic tumbler with an inch of wine in it.

Slater frowned. "Come on, man—fill it up."

Eyeing him, the bartender obliged, topping it off.

Slater dropped a dollar in his tip jar and drank deeply as he made his way toward Doris and Albert. The walls of the gallery were gray and blank; the art seemed to be a series of plaster busts mounted at chest height on simple pedestals. They were realistic representations of people, eyes open, unsmiling, and formally posed.

Doris spotted him as he approached. "Here's my handsome son," she said, squeezing him around the shoulder.

She was shorter than Slater and petite, and lately she was letting some gray show in her dark hair. Slater stooped to kiss her hello, then begrudgingly greeted Albert. Dumpy and with a comb-over that wasn't fooling anyone, the guy was fairly new on the scene, and Slater didn't trust him one bit, not least of all because he drove a doll car—a stupid little Boxster. Stuck to Albert's shirt was a sticker of a slice of pepperoni, and Doris had the oak leaf.

"You didn't invite Conrad?" Slater asked her. "I thought you two might be conspiring on something tonight."

"It's just us," Doris said. "I see you got yourself a drink."

"I need to drink to make you two tolerable."

Doris laughed. "Have you had a look at the art?"

"It's interesting stuff," Slater said, glancing around.

"It looks like the Roman art at the Vatican," Albert said. "This stuff is realistic like that. They're actual portraits of people, not like Rodin. Have you seen his stuff at LACMA? They're way sloppier. Impressionistic, I guess you'd say."

Doris nodded, listening to him. "I wonder

what these pieces are supposed to mean."

"Come on, Doris," Slater said. "I know you can do this. You don't have to play dumb just because your boyfriend is."

Albert scowled. "I'm a lot of things, but I am not dumb. It's a huge amount of work to become a surgeon. I was in school for a decade."

Slater gave him the once-over. It was worrying that he was feeling emboldened to stand up to Slater. That was new.

"Nothing personal, Albert," he said, "but that doesn't exactly sound smart." Looking to Doris, he waved at the room. "Well?"

She stepped over to a nearby bust, a woman with short hair, a curved nose, hollow pupils creating a realistic gaze, like in classical statuary.

"All right," Doris said finally. "Maybe the artist did this because no one else is doing it—forging a new style by using a classical form. Rodin changed things, and maybe this artist is working to change it again."

"OK," Slater said.

"Maybe it's a comment on how intangible art has become. The true human form is about as essential as it gets." She turned back to them, gesturing at the room. "Or maybe it's a reaction to all the electronic representations of everything. A 3-D plaster bust is never going to make sense inside your cell phone, but here you can walk all the way around it."

"Yes," Slater said emphatically. "That's the analytical mind I know. I was worried it was getting atrophied from neglect." He looked pointedly at Albert. "She worked as an educator, not someone who memorized tables of numbers and lists of Latin nomenclature."

"Medicine is analytical sometimes," Albert protested.

"Like a toaster is analytical," Slater said flatly. "Doctors are like toasters, but with less social skills."

"Play nice," Doris said firmly, squeezing his arm.

Albert sighed and looked around. "Maybe all these faces are just people that the artist loves."

Slater scoffed, but Doris said, "I like that idea," and looped her arm under his, cuddling up to him.

They spent a little more time in the gallery, strolling around and looking at the faces up close, not lingering for the activity that necessitated the stickers, whatever that was going to be. When they left, Doris suggested they go to an ice cream place nearby, and they walked the few blocks together.

After she'd assessed the options in the display case, Doris said, "Get me a scoop of the lavender," and went to the restroom.

Slater ordered and watched as the clerk

scooped ice cream into little cups.

"I'm not going anywhere, you know," Albert said, standing beside him with his arms folded. "I love your mother."

Slater glanced at him sidelong. "Your feelings are of no concern to me at all."

Albert didn't reply right away. "I'm not afraid of you," he said finally.

"Good. That means you won't be on your guard when I come for you."

Doris came back as the clerk handed the little cups across the counter. Slater had ordered the lone vegan variety on offer, instantly regretting it once he'd tasted it, a powerful blast of cardamom and little else. He dropped the cup in the trash and sat with Doris and Albert as they ate.

"You look tired," Doris said, gesturing with her little spoon. "What are you working on these days?"

"Some people in the Miracle Mile hearing ghosts in their apartment."

"There's no such thing," Albert said.

"I stayed there and heard it, but I can't find the source. I think it might be the upstairs neighbor."

"Have you thought any more about taking a break from the booze?" Doris said, holding his gaze.

"Where did that come from?" Slater demanded. "I don't need a break, because I don't have a problem." Doris didn't reply, and Slater studied her for a moment. "You're always trying to fix me. That parade of shrinks all through my childhood. I'm surprised you didn't invite one of them along tonight."

"I tried," she said, raising her eyebrows, "but they were all at a symposium in Vienna."

Albert chuckled, and Slater shot him a look.

"Remember that one who wanted me to cry for half an hour every day?" Slater demanded. "And I'm the one who's crazy."

"Nobody thinks you're crazy," Doris said, tapping his forearm. "But it never hurts to talk to people—share ideas, compare notes."

"You mean I should go to an AA meeting."

"Maybe," she said. "Whatever works."

Slater reached for her empty cup, and taking it, stood up and took it to the trash.

"I have to go," he said, and bent down to kiss her. "Love you." Looking to Albert, he frowned, and said evenly, "Albert."

* * *

Walking toward Fifth Street, he wanted nothing more than to go home to sleep, but he wasn't going to leave his car on the street overnight unnecessarily. He found the stop for the Wilshire express bus and waited with the small crowd that had accumulated, trudging on board when the articulated behemoth arrived and finding a seat by the rear door.

At the first stop, in the Financial District, he watched the commuters stepping on, more out of the habit of doing surveillance than any real interest. But then he saw a familiar face—June from the Camellia building boarded, wearing the same outfit she'd had on when she left this morning. As she walked by, scanning for a seat, she glanced at him, but there was no spark of recognition. Of course she wouldn't remember him; there was no reason she would. The only time she'd seen Slater, he'd been up a ladder outside her apartment, and this was a completely different context. It seemed like a long time ago, but it was just this morning when he'd watched the video of her leaving, and she still looked sharp after a long workday. That alone was an impressive accomplishment for someone who lived out of garbage bags. The lawyers she worked with knew about her lead foot, as Conrad said they helped her challenge her speeding citations, but he'd bet money no one knew what the inside of her apartment looked like.

June got off at the stop in the Miracle Mile closest to the Camellia building, and Slater trailed her for several blocks. But she wasn't part of this case, not really, and there was no point in shadowing her, risking recognition. He turned up a side street a block before the one where her building was. His car was near the corner, just a few steps to walk back to it from the cross street.

Striding up the quiet block, just before the corner, he spotted two shaggy guys standing next to a van with Missouri plates. Not homeless, he decided as he approached, so probably not a threat. Baggy clothes and lots of hair—maybe they were musicians.

As he passed, the lanky one with the beard asked, "Hey, man, can I ask you a favor?"

Slater met his eye but didn't break his stride. "I can't help you."

"You didn't even hear what I have to say," he snapped.

"That's unlikely to change anything," Slater said, stopping and turning to face him, "but what do you want?"

"Why are people so rude around here?"

"You stopped me to ask me that?" Slater demanded. "There are sixty thousand homeless people within ten miles of this street. When someone around here asks for help, it always means 'Give me money.'"

"That's not what I was going to ask."

"Then what do you want?" Slater said intently, raising his voice.

"I locked myself out of my van."

"So call the auto club."

"My phone's inside."

"Why would you think I'd know how to break into a car?" Slater demanded. "Do I look like a car thief?"

He looked him up and down, frowning thoughtfully. "Well …"

The other guy, shorter than his comrade and thick, his greasy hair in a ponytail, spoke for the first time. "I like your little sticker. It's pretty gay."

Slater had forgotten he was wearing it, but tapped it and said, "Thank you."

He frowned. "That's not what I meant."

"I didn't think so," Slater said. "Funny that you knuckleheads are calling me rude."

The one with the beard told his friend, "Just let it go, man."

"This is an oak leaf," Slater said, taking a step toward them. "It's symbolic of strength. My mother and I both got one this evening."

Ponytail scoffed. "What, are you nine years old?"

"I hoped you'd say something like that," Slater said, and stepped toward him, punching him in the nose, lightning fast. He stepped back casually to see how he'd react, fists at the ready.

Ponytail hadn't expected that, grabbing his nose. "That's assault," he cried, his tone shrill. "You assaulted me. I'm calling the cops."

"You can't," Slater said flatly. "You locked your phone in your van."

The bearded one stepped back, wary, toward the front of his vehicle, but Ponytail moved toward Slater now, rage in his eyes. Maybe he was high, because his reaction time seemed sluggish—Slater struck him on the jaw and body-slammed him onto the van before he was able to throw a punch. Grabbing his wrist and twisting him around, Slater pinned him against the vehicle.

"Stand down," Slater said, through gritted teeth, one hand on his collar, the other pushing his wrist up his back.

The guy went slack, knowing he was outmatched. Slater stepped away, watching them both.

"When the next person comes by, just ask them to call the auto club," he said, throwing his hands in the air, and walked toward the corner, listening closely in case one of them decided to escalate and come after him. But no one was following him, he saw as he turned the corner.

The Thunderbird was where he'd left it, thankfully unmolested, and he climbed in, feeling his muscles start to relax just feeling the low thrum of the engine.

Traffic was light, making for an easy drive back to Westlake along Sixth Street. He knew what was waiting for him, anticipated that golden embrace all the way home.

Stepping into his kitchen, he locked the door and pulled open the cupboard, finding the fifth of bourbon and drinking from the bottle, relishing the burn. Filling a tumbler, he dropped in an ice cube and stretched out on the sofa, kicking off his boots. Unconsciousness loomed as soon as he closed his eyes, so he felt for the tumbler on the carpet and took a deep drink before that happened. Smiling to himself, he slipped into the inviting comfort of sleep.

EIGHT

Strident ringing started him awake. He looked at the room, not remembering how he'd gotten into bed, not sure how he got naked. His phone, he realized, and scrabbled for it on the bedside table. It was Andy, the self-declared computer whiz.

"I didn't find much," Andy said, "so my rates are … reduced. You just have to blow me."

"What did you find?" Slater asked.

"You'll have to come over here and submit payment first."

"Give me half an hour," he said, and ended the call.

After he splashed water on his face, he ate a spoonful of peanut butter and fished a few olives out of the jar in the fridge, standing over the garbage to spit out the pits. Matías's delivery uniform was still on the bedroom floor, and he folded it up, stuffing it into his satchel.

He backed his car out of the garage and drove the short distance to Andy's loft, across the chasm of the 110 freeway into downtown. Happily there was room in the surface lot next to his building, and it wasn't insanely overpriced.

When Slater knocked on the door, it took him a minute to answer, but when he pulled it open, his hair unkempt and wild and perfect, Andy broke into a big smile. Such a beautiful man.

"What have you got for me?" Slater asked, stepping inside.

"My big dick," he said, turning and walking unevenly into the room, and then looked back, frowning. "What's … so funny?"

"I like your unpolished side," Slater said, unable to conceal his amusement.

"Payment first," Andy said. "On your knees, son."

"Are you sure you want to be standing for this?"

Andy dropped onto the bed, and Slater knelt in front of him, taking charge of unzipping his pants, and took him into his mouth. Andy rapidly got hard, and as he got close, he pounded his palms on Slater's head, then pushed him off when he finally came.

Slater would have been content with that, but when he got up and sat on the bed with him, Andy grabbed Slater's belt, eventually getting it unbuckled. Slater helped him undo his jeans, and Andy kissed him and grabbed his cock, stroking it until he came too.

Afterward Slater put his arm over his eyes, catching his breath.

"Your rates are too low," he said finally. "Sex is basically free—you should ask for money."

"Sex with you is more valuable than … the basic version," Andy said. "We should do it regularly."

"Man, don't do that."

"Do what?" he demanded.

"Like me," Slater said, not looking at him. "Don't like me. I'm not who you think I am."

Andy sat up. "You don't appreciate the spazziness, is that it? The slow walk, the slow talk? You're just playing tourist in my world?"

"I never sleep with anyone twice," Slater said, glaring at him. "You're already an exception to that. I don't need a freaking boyfriend."

"That's not what I said I wanted. You're projecting your own … bullshit onto me."

Slater took a deep breath and sat up. "What did you find with my target?"

Andy zipped his pants and shifted to the end

of the bed. "I couldn't get into the email, but I got his phone records."

"How did you manage that?"

"Don't ask. It's a data file, so there's not actually anything physical to hand over. Give me your email address, and I'll send it to you later today."

Slater rose and pulled a business card out of his jeans, handing it to him. "I'm going to go."

"Damn right you are," he said, scowling and snagging the card. "Go on—piss off out of my place."

Slater scoffed. "You're a piece of work, Andy."

He let himself out and walked back to his car. The guy was such a compelling amalgam of hard and soft. But no way did he want to get involved with him—he'd wind up pushing him around in that freaking wheelchair. That was a stupid reason not to connect with him, Slater knew that. Still, he wasn't going to get sticky with Andy.

Driving the few blocks to his office, he thought about Cash. The guy hadn't contacted him, but it had been a day or so since they'd met. If Slater reached out now, it would probably conform with the arcane messed-up courtship rules that squares used. Riding the elevator up to his office, he found the place dark and empty, and he set his satchel on his desk, dropping into his chair and heaving his feet up, phone in hand, thinking through what might best elicit a response. Finally he texted Cash:

> Just ate a microwave burrito from a Japanese convenience store. Does that make me the worst of the non-Hispanic Hispanics?

Checking on Conrad, the tracking app said he was at home, out in the Valley. Slater dialed his cell number.

"Hey Slater," he answered.

"Are you at your station?"

"I'm off today."

"Seriously?" Slater said. "Well, fuck you, then, and stop wasting my time."

As he hung up, he heard Max coming in the front door. He stuck his head in Slater's office, wearing the seersucker again today, his necktie loose at his collar.

"How was sleeping at Mike and Jessica's?" Slater asked.

Max dropped into the chair in front of the desk. "I love that bed."

"I didn't actually try it—I slept on the sofa. Did you hear the ghosts?"

"They started at three thirty, right on schedule. First the baby, and then a woman crying."

"Interesting," Slater said. "I never heard that one."

"Later she whispered 'Leave this place.' It went on for about twenty minutes."

"Did it feel supernatural?"

"Not in the slightest," Max said. "It felt programmed and choreographed, like a show in Vegas."

"If it starts at the same time every night, it might be like that—some kind of automated system."

"I couldn't figure out where it was coming from either. It seemed to be all around my head."

"That's what I thought too—no specific source."

"I was looking at the dead staircase," Max said. "I feel like it has something to do with it. Did the landlord build a new floor over it, or is it just boarded over? Maybe that's how the guys upstairs are feeding the sound into 302."

"Still, how could they make it omnidirectional? It doesn't make sense."

Max sighed. "Did you see last night's activity? June came home once, and Cash came home twice."

"I saw the first Cash go in. When he did, he tripped an alarm."

"I noticed that. I guess that means we're not going in there."

"Maybe there's another way," Slater said, and flipped open his satchel, pulling out Matías's delivery uniform.

Max held up the shirt and fingered the delivery company's logo embroidered on it. "What's this for?"

"I had an idea. We get another camera from the Russians and put it in a box addressed to Jessica or Mike in 302. You wear the uniform and take it to 402. I can't, because one of them knows me. You might get a look inside if they open the door, and if not, you just leave it there."

"Why would they open the box if it's addressed to a neighbor?"

"Who checks the shipping label?" Slater said. "If a package is on your doorstep, wouldn't you just rip it open?"

"Not unless I was expecting something. Why not just address it to Cash?"

"They'd be suspicious of that. Once you open it and see it's not something you ordered, you'd definitely check the shipping label. A delivery guy leaving a box at the wrong door isn't too hard to believe, and it wouldn't make you paranoid. Some people would take it downstairs to the right person, but not everyone. The best-case scenario is if they decide not to return it—we get eyes inside."

Max nodded, considering that. "Freaking great idea," he said finally, and picked up the shirt again, holding it across his shoulders. "This will fit me, no problem. What do you need me to do to set it up?"

"I'll print the shipping label, and ask the Russians about a camera. Maybe you could get a box and some packing tape?"

"Done," he said, standing up. "There's a place within walking distance, on Maple."

Watching him leave, Slater had to grin. He loved that about Max—his enthusiasm, always ready to do the work.

Digging around online, he found images of the shipping label that Matías's company used, and altered it by superimposing Jessica's name and address, then printed it out. As he pulled it off the printer, there was a knock at the door. Slater frowned. No one ever came here unannounced. Locking his computer with a quick keystroke, he set the label face down on his desk and went to the door.

Standing there was a woman, maybe not yet thirty, in a summery blouse and trousers. Her intricate hairstyle looked expensive, which might mean she had money, although a lot of black women spent big on their hair. Draped around her neck was a bundle of fine gold strands, glittering warm against her dark skin.

"What can I do for you, sister?"

She smiled. "You must be Max's partner."

"Might be," Slater said. "And you are?"

"Vanessa. I'm Jessica's sister. You were researching the ghosts in her apartment while she's back east."

"You're Vanessa?"

She arched her eyebrows. "You look surprised."

"No," he lied.

"It's Slater, right? Is Max here?"

"He'll be back any minute," he said, stepping aside to let her enter. "Have you been here before?"

"First time," she said, glancing around the cramped front room.

"That's Max's office," Slater said, gesturing to the doorway. "He's got the window."

Vanessa stepped inside. "This is kind of depressing."

Slater sighed, forcing civility. "We're new at running an office—most of our work is in the field. We might upgrade from here someday."

Glancing down into Max's wastebasket, she said, "Take-out junk food wrappers and a soda cup. I guess you can learn a lot about a man from his garbage."

Slater folded his arms, watching her from the doorway. "In our business we don't always get time to eat well."

She stepped behind the desk, close to the window, and peered out. "You can almost see the sky." Turning back to him, she said, "I know what you're thinking—Jessica has a much lighter complexion than me, and I'm much darker. We're half-sisters."

"Interesting," Slater said, "but that's not what I was thinking. Where did you meet Max?"

"I'm a grad student at Cal-Tech. I met him in a coffee place near there."

"OK," Slater said evenly. It was surprising Cal-Tech didn't have an injunction to prevent Max even driving by and lowering the average IQ of the neighborhood. "Can I ask what you see in him?"

Vanessa smiled. "I know he's a little older than me. That must seem odd to some people. He's strong, and he's sincere, and he doesn't lie to me." She flipped her hair back with her hand. "Maybe there's something of my father in him. He was a hard-ass too. It's a thing, right—we're attracted to people like our parents. Do you date women like your mother?"

Slater scowled. "I only date guys."

"Right—I think Max mentioned that. Well, do you date guys like your father?"

"It's hard to remember him. He died when I was thirteen."

"Oh, I'm so sorry. That's an awful age to lose a parent."

"It was pretty gross," Slater agreed.

The front door flew open, and Max came in, a couple of flat corrugated boxes under one arm, a shopping bag dangling from the other.

"I got bubble wrap too," he said, dumping them on the desk in the front office.

"This is quite the place," Vanessa said, stepping into the room.

"You're here," Max said, beaming at the sight of her. "So this is it—the nexus of all the action. I know it's a little rough around the edges, but we like it, don't we?"

"We do," Slater said.

"I guess I'd say it's atmospheric," she said.

Max looked at Slater. "She's at a private school with an endowment bigger than Switzerland's. Her personal office is the size of this whole floor. All the plumbing is gold-plated."

"Not quite," she said, and smiled.

Max waved at the room. "Well, this is how working people do things."

Vanessa turned to Slater. "Do you mind if I borrow Max for lunch?"

"By all means," Slater said.

Following them to the door, he watched as they left, Max's arm around her waist.

Sitting down at his desk, he had to grin. Vanessa was smart, beautiful, and had resources. Max must have something going on that he just couldn't see.

What had Max said about the dead stairs? He'd wondered how the landlord had sealed up the gap. Turning to his computer, he searched for details on how floors were constructed, and how they'd been built in the 1920s. There was a lot of information to dig through, but he got a sense of it, and then looked up how to fill in a stair-well-size hole in a floor. Surprisingly, removing staircases seemed to be a common enough renovation project, and several do-it-yourself sites explained the process in detail.

All of them advised bridging the gap by adding joists, securely attached to the existing flooring. But that meant there would be a lot of dead space left between the new floorboards and the ceiling below. It didn't make sense to break through Mike and Jessica's ceiling to check, but maybe he could determine whether Cash and his double were up to something, using that space. Max's stepladder was still there—Slater could examine the ceiling, at least, thump on it, check whether the drywall was loose or solidly integrated.

Looking at his email, he found a message from Andy, with a document attached. It was a long list of numbers in a series of columns, and he spent a minute trying to parse it. Each line was a phone call, he saw—a numeric date, start and end times listed in military format, then a phone number. This was a log of Cash's phone calls. Scanning the date column, the newest ones were yesterday, the oldest three months back.

Digging through it seemed like a lot of work, but there was another email from Andy, with another attachment and a note from him:

> This is the same data but with a bit of formatting. I added a column that calculates the duration of each call. You can click on any phone number to search the Web for that number. It's also sortable by column, so you can group the same number together.

That was incredibly helpful, he realized, clicking open the spreadsheet. Andy really needed to charge money for this kind of work.

Sorted by phone number, it was easier to see that Cash had actually talked to a lot fewer people than the long list implied. Slater clicked on a few of the most frequently called, which brought up a Web search, as promised. There was no information about most of them, meaning they were probably personal cell numbers. But one was linked to a Thai restaurant. Checking the address, it was in the Miracle Mile. The food must be good—Cash called them several times a month.

Clicking through more of the numbers brought little insight, until one of them came up as "In your contacts: Glendale Eastern Imports." He picked up his phone to check. It was the number he used for Svetlana, and Cash had called her four times in the last few weeks. That was unexpected, and a little worrying—he needed to talk to her. He sighed and texted Svetlana:

Can I drop by later today?

A moment later came her reply:

I do nothing but work. You know where to find me.

NINE

After he locked his computer, he slung on his satchel and headed down to his car. Mike and Jessica's ceiling first, he decided, and then Svetlana. The navigation app had him take Olympic, which was moving fluidly at this time of day, and soon he was pulling up across the street from the Camellia building. Lots of the neighborhood residents must be at work, as there was plenty of parking.

Just before he climbed out, his phone buzzed, and he pulled it out to check. The camera app had picked up movement on the fourth floor. Watching the video, Cash stepped out the door to 402, wearing a bulky backpack and a red-and-white checked shirt, pausing to lock the deadbolt. As he stepped out of frame on the screen,

Slater looked up at movement across the street. Here was Cash walking out between the jasmine and the sword ferns, headed down the sidewalk toward Wilshire. At least it looked like Cash—they'd both gone into 402 last night, so there was a chance it was the other one.

Should he follow him? Yesterday he hadn't learned much doing that, but at least he'd been able to hit on the guy. In his side mirror, Slater watched as Cash stopped partway down the block, between parked cars. A minute later he reappeared, straddling a motorcycle, nosing it into the street. A helmet with a black visor obscured his face, but it was the same shirt, the same gray backpack. Max hadn't been able to keep up with him yesterday, so maybe it wasn't worth it. But the bike pulled out and went right past Slater to the end of the block, waiting to turn left. That made the decision easy.

Slater pulled into the street, waiting for the light and following the bike as it made the left. Moving fast, he was blocks ahead by the time Slater caught up, pushing the Thunderbird hard. A left on Fairfax took them both into heavy traffic, and Cash got stuck—a bus paralleling a heavy truck meant there wasn't room for the bike to split the lanes, and he had to crawl along at the same pace as everyone else. A few blocks later, the truck fell back, and the bike whipped in front of it, left and around the bus. Idling in the right lane, Slater assumed he'd lost him, but then saw the flash of the red shirt on the bike, navigating a long driveway farther up the block—he was going into the Grove, a massive shopping mall.

The bus rumbled past the driveway, and Slater pulled in. There was no sign of the bike, but he'd been headed straight into the parking structure, and with any luck, he might catch him walking out. Pulling up to the valet desk on the ground floor, Slater hopped out and gestured impatiently for a claim ticket from the attendant, snatching it and walking fast toward the elevator lobby. Cash or his double would have parked on a higher floor, hopefully giving Slater enough time to catch up.

The place was bustling, as it always was, and Slater scanned the crowd, looking for the red checked shirt among the sea of bodies as he walked out of the structure into the open-air mall. There he was—not far away, across the courtyard. With so many people around, the guy wouldn't notice him even if it was Cash, even if they had met yesterday. Slater followed as he stepped into a department store, heading up the escalator. He seemed to know exactly where he was going, and as Slater reached the top, he was already at the customer service counter.

A few yards away but within earshot, Slater

stood behind a rack of clothes and flipped through the garments—women's blouses, he realized—straining to hear the conversation at the counter. Cash had his back to him, so he didn't pick up most of what he said, but the clerk he was dealing with was clearly audible. Cash pulled a leather jacket out of the backpack and set it on the counter.

"The tags are intact," the clerk said, looking it over, "so I can issue the refund in cash." After scanning the tags on the jacket with a hand-held device, and then a minute of gazing at her computer screen, she tore off a length of register tape that had spewed out of the terminal, handing it to him, and then started counting out bills—hundreds at first, Slater saw, glancing over at them. He lost count, but there were at least a dozen before she switched to twenties. It wasn't surprising—in a place like this, that jacket could easily cost two grand. Cash folded the bills in half and quickly pocketed them, walking away, toward the down escalator.

Rather than heading back toward the parking lot, once he was out of the store Cash walked toward Fairfax, along the driveway and out of the mall. It was harder to tail him out here on the street, with so few pedestrians, but the bulky backpack and the red shirt stood out. Slater stayed back a block or so, tailing him as he made his way north. Where the hell was he going?

Once they were past Melrose, the neighborhood was a lot denser, with narrow storefronts lining both sides. When Slater was a kid, this stretch of retail had been oriented to the neighborhood's Orthodox families who had to walk everywhere on Shabbat. Today it had gone upscale and trendy, with hip boutiques, eateries, and pubs. One of the few remnants of its past incarnation was the deli where he'd bought the rugelach for Grace. Cash could have easily ridden his motorcycle here; why had he walked all this way?

Losing sight of him, Slater quickened his pace, glancing into the storefronts along the stretch where he'd disappeared. He wasn't in the menswear boutique, or the sushi bar, or the automated gourmet breakfast-cereal dispensary. Scanning the street, he saw no sign of the red shirt. Had he jaywalked and gone into a shop on the other side? But then he caught sight of him, inside a store that had no sign above it, nothing in the window except brown paper taped across the bottom half of the panes. What he could see inside told him exactly what it was—a sneaker exchange. Cash was standing between stacks of shoeboxes, talking to a guy with a riot of dreads, wearing a baggy track suit and a blue ball cap the wrong way around.

There seemed to be a sizeable demographic

that was willing to pay absurd prices for rare sneakers. Manufacturers fed the scarcity by making small lots and charging top dollar, but the real profit was in the resale market, and Slater had seen several of these places pop up around the city. Walking past, he stopped a little farther up the block, in front of a luxury eyewear place, feigning interest in the window display.

People strolled by behind him, talking loud to be heard over the rumble of the traffic, and eventually Cash stepped out of the sneaker place, his backpack now flat and empty.

Slater hustled back to the shop's entrance and ducked inside. The guy with the ball cap was sitting on a bench between the stacks of shoeboxes, holding a yellow sneaker and studying the tread. As Slater approached him, he set the shoe in the box beside him with its mate and covered it with the lid, as if it was something illicit, or a treasure not suitable for public display.

"Did you just buy those?" Slater asked.

The guy frowned. "What's it to you?"

"I might be interested. What are they worth?"

He looked at Slater's boots. "These won't fit you, bruh."

"They're not for me. Can you tell me what you're asking for them, at least?"

"You know that expression, 'If you have to ask, you can't afford it?' I don't think you can afford these. They're extremely rare. Only seventeen pairs were ever made."

Slater put his hands on his hips. "The ballpark, then."

"I just spent twenty-eight on these, cash money, so I'd have to get at least four. I'm not selling, though."

"Twenty-eight hundred?" Slater asked. "For one pair of shoes? That's the stupidest fucking thing I've heard in weeks."

As Slater turned to leave, the guy shouted after him, "Hey—fuck you."

Ignoring him, Slater hustled out to the sidewalk, looking for Cash's red shirt. When he'd stepped out of the sneaker place he'd turned south, and Slater saw him in that direction, farther ahead, just crossing the boulevard, headed back toward the mall.

Slater got closer as Cash turned into the driveway, then walked back into the crowd of shoppers. Not wasting any time, or even looking in the store windows, he went directly to the parking structure. Most people took the escalators up to the higher levels, but Cash stepped into the empty elevator lobby. It wouldn't be that odd to run into an acquaintance here, Slater reasoned, one of the busiest places for miles around, and rather than dropping the tail, as he probably should have, he walked into the elevator lobby.

At that moment a car arrived with a *ding,* and Cash stepped toward the doors, waited for its occupants to file off before he boarded. But was it Cash? This close up, it looked exactly like him— the same natty haircut, the same eyes. Slater followed him on, punching the button for the floor one level up from the one Cash had pressed. As the door closed, with just the two of them inside, Slater turned and spoke.

"Hey—how are you?" he said, grinning at him, and then reaching for his hair, gently pushing it across his forehead.

He ducked and stepped away. "Dude, what the hell?"

Slater frowned. "You don't remember me?"

"Hell, no," he said, glaring at Slater, but uncertainty furrowed his brow.

"You look like someone I know," Slater said. "A lot. You've got a doppelgänger out there."

"I guess everybody probably does," he said, calmer now, stepping off as the elevator door opened. He stopped to look back, hands on the shoulder straps of his backpack, studying Slater.

Slater raised a hand to wave as the door closed. There had been no spark of recognition, meaning this was definitely the other twin. From what he'd seen, they were thoroughly identical— no way could he tell them apart.

Getting off on the higher floor, Slater walked

along the row of parked cars to the corner of the structure and took the stairs down to the ground level, walking up to the valet desk and handing the clerk his claim ticket. The fee was exorbitant for the privilege to park at a shopping mall, but he knew he had to rationalize it as a business expense, and soon he had his car back.

The ceiling in 302 could wait, he decided—he really wanted to talk to Svetlana, to find out how she was connected to Cash and his twin. Glendale was a long schlep on surface streets, and Slater settled in for the drive, mulling over what he'd seen.

The whole outing felt shady, returning an unused garment and then selling a pair of shoes, both for excessive amounts of cash. The guy was walking around with four or five grand in his pockets, and he'd only made a couple of stops. Who knew where he was obtaining the stuff, or what he was actually doing, but it definitely smelled like a scam.

Leaving the Thunderbird parked in front of Glendale Eastern Imports, he walked around to the alley and waited to enter, getting the usual brief pat-down by the taciturn dark-suited guy. Svetlana was at the bench in the workroom, wearing a top printed in riotous yellow and orange flowers. She turned around to look at him over her glasses.

"You like the cameras Garik made?" she asked.

"It's all working perfectly, like it always does," he said.

She nodded, satisfied. "And you like Garik?"

"He seems like a nice guy."

"Good," she said, not hiding a grin. She probably knew they'd slept together, he realized.

"So what do you need today?" she asked.

"A camera hidden in something that might get left on a shelf."

"We have lots of those," she said, rising from her stool and languorously arching her back.

When she held her wrist to the sensor beside the inner door, the lock snapped open, and Slater followed her into the next room. This space was more about storage than fabrication, with tall shelves laden with electronic components, wiring, and rows of plastic storage tubs. In one corner was a set of shelves that looked different, like it belonged in a thrift shop, stacked with junky-looking figurines, clocks, and toys.

"We call these *tsatska*," Svetlana said.

"Sounds like the same word in English," he said. "Tchotchke."

"How about this?" She picked up an ornate boxy clock, gilt leaves curling around the corners, Gothic roman numerals on the dial. It wouldn't be out of place on a mantel at Versailles.

"What are my other options?" Slater asked.

"Jesus is quite fashionable," she said, pointing out a shoulders-up figurine, his head tilted to one side, sadly looking skyward, blood dripping from the ring of thorns puncturing his forehead. It was hard to imagine where the camera lens would be.

Slater pointed to a porcelain statue of a stylized cat, white with red ears, one paw in the air. "What about this one?"

"Good choice," Svetlana said. "Japanese. It's beckoning to bring money. Shopkeepers love them—they always put them behind the register, so you can keep an eye on the transactions." She pulled it down and pointed out the black beads on the cat's collar. "The lens is here."

Walking back into the workshop, she unceremoniously popped off the cat's head.

"You want to go wireless?"

"It has to work over the cell network," Slater said.

Svetlana sat at the workbench and put on her glasses, adjusting something inside the cat. Finally she waved him over.

"Turn it on here," she said, pointing out an almost invisible toggle switch recessed in the cat's collar. "I put in a big battery, fully charged, so it should last at least five days."

After she reattached the head, she tucked the statue into a white plastic take-out bag with THANK YOU printed on it in red lettering. It was heavy, Slater thought, taking it from her.

"How much?" he asked.

"Including connection to your camera account, four hundred."

Slater nodded and set the cat on the floor, pulling out his wad of cash and peeling off four C-notes.

Svetlana frowned as she took the cash. "You always try to negotiate. Why not today?"

"I'm worried I might be interfering with your business," he said, meeting her eye. "I wanted to ask you about that. In my work I'm investigating someone who's connected to you."

"To me?" she said, eyeing him intently. "How do you know this?"

"I got his phone log. He called you four times in the last few weeks."

"Who is this person?" she said slowly, holding his gaze.

"His name is Cash. He lives in the Miracle Mile. I don't want to take him down if he's working for you."

"I don't know any Cash. What phone number did he call?"

"The same one I use." Slater pulled out his phone and read off Cash's number.

Svetlana turned to her laptop, clacking at the keyboard and scanning a spreadsheet.

"This is Logan's number," she said finally.

"I've heard him use that name—that's the guy." Either Cash was using two names, or Logan was the twin he'd tailed to the mall and the sneaker exchange.

She turned back to him. "Logan is a client. Small-time. Not that important to me." She threw a hand in the air. "Go ahead, take him out."

"Down," Slater said. "I might have to take him down, not take him out."

"This means disable him, not killing, right?"

"Exactly."

Svetlana shrugged. "Either way. He's not a tech client like you. I help him get inputs for his business that are difficult to source."

"I don't suppose you can tell me what those inputs are?" Slater said.

"I don't ask what you do with these devices," she said. "Extend me the same courtesy, OK?"

"I had to try, at least," he said, picking up the bag with the cat sculpture. Walking to the door, he said, *"Spasiba,"* the attempt eliciting a cackle from Svetlana, and he waved good-bye as the lock snapped open for him.

Whatever it was that Cash, or Logan, or the pair of them was buying from her, he thought, walking back around to his car, it was illicit— people didn't come here for things they could get at the hardware store.

TEN

On the drive back downtown, his phone rang, and he recognized the number right away—he'd just recited it to Svetlana.

"This is Cash," he said, when Slater picked up. "You texted me today."

"I remember," Slater said. "The non-Hispanic Hispanic."

"So I have to be out of my place tonight. Do you want to get together?"

"Definitely. You want to come over? I live in Westlake."

"I was thinking we could meet at a coffeehouse in Hollywood."

"I don't really do dates," Slater said, "and small talk, and all that."

"It's not a date. I have to be there. We can skip the small talk and go back to your place after."

It sounded like a complete waste of time, but this wasn't a regular hookup—this was for work.

"Fine," Slater said.

"The place is called Madre Mía. It's on Sunset in Hollywood."

They planned when to meet, and after he hung up, Slater thumped the steering wheel.

"Yes," he said emphatically. Sending that stupid text had worked.

Traffic was sluggish at the end of the business day, and when he parked across from his building, the attendants were already gone. With his new acquisition in hand, he went up to the office and built one of the cardboard boxes Max had bought, and attached the label with Jessica's name on it. Leaving the top of the box open, he draped Matías's delivery uniform on it, then set the cat statue beside it, on top of the bubble wrap, facing the door, so the wide-eyed feline would greet Max when he came in. Slater sent him a quick text:

> Package ready, on my desk. Activate the power switch on the back of the collar before delivery.

There was time to eat and clean up his place before he was due to meet Cash, and he stopped at a *taquería* on the way, ordering a rice-and-bean burrito to take with him. Once he'd parked and climbed the stairs to his apartment, he ate it over the sink, then hid his satchel behind the sofa, stowing the bourbon out of sight in a kitchen cupboard.

Pulling his shirt off and finding a clean one—black satin felt right for a night out—he buttoned it in front of the bathroom mirror, running a hand through his hair. He didn't need to shave again, he decided. Cash wouldn't be put off by a day's stubble.

Without traffic, Hollywood was only a few minutes away, but it was still early evening, and his navigation app sent him on the sluggish 101. Crawling along in the right lane, he turned on his headlights as the daylight faded, and before long he was nosing the Thunderbird to the curb on a side street, under a sprawling ficus, just a few minutes' walk back to Madre Mía.

Climbing out, Slater stopped to study the tree, a species so reviled these days because its thick shallow roots heaved the concrete sidewalks and broke the curbs.

A woman with short hair, pushing a massive stroller on the sidewalk, asked, "Don't you hate those things? The pavement is a mess."

Slater looked at her. "You won't have to harbor that hostility for much longer. This one will be dead in a couple years."

She frowned. "That sounds ominous. How do you know that?"

"See those gnarly things?" he said, pointing to the trunk. "Those are cankers full of bot fungus. They're killing the tree—and there's no cure."

"Is the city planning to replace them?"

"I don't know. If they do, you're going to like the next tree a lot less."

Slater walked away, toward the boulevard and Madre Mía. The place was crowded, considering it was almost dark outside and they sold java, but soon he figured out why—at the back of the space was a low stage, with a cello resting on a rack, and three music stands with books splayed open on them, but no mikes or other amplification that he could see. There was going to be a performance. Slater scanned the tables but couldn't see Cash among the youthful crowd.

At the counter he ordered a decaf soy latte, and while he was waiting for it, the cellist stepped onto the stage and took her seat, soon joined by a violinist, who stood with her instrument in hand. Both of them were dressed casually, the cellist in trousers and a blouse and the violinist in a print dress, and both looked Latin, maybe in their twenties. Then Cash appeared, stepping up onto the stage with them. In his hand was a gleaming silver rod—a flute, Slater realized. Cash had invited him to watch him perform. Slater took his paper cup and stood near the front window with the other overflow spectators.

Cash was wearing jeans but also a dressy white tuxedo shirt and a black bow tie. Catching sight of Slater, he grinned and gave him a little nod.

When the violinist spoke, attention in the room focused on her. "Thanks for coming," she said, waiting for them to quiet down. "We don't usually play together, but I hope you like what you hear."

With that, the crowd clapped politely, the violinist notched the instrument under her chin and raised her bow, and Cash hefted his flute, eyes on his music stand. They launched into a piece that was upbeat but clearly something classical. The music seemed grander than just three instruments, filling the room, perhaps a reflection of their level of skill, although Slater couldn't really assess that, except in his impression that the three of them sounded great together. He admired Cash, standing there so intently focused on the instrument, his lips pursed over the mouthpiece, swaying a little from time to time, the tip of the flute bobbing as he worked the keys.

When it ended, everyone applauded, and Cash beamed, basking in the attention.

"You have to love Haydn," the woman

standing beside Slater said, clearly pleased with the performance, her eyes bright.

"I don't know her," Slater said. "Is she the violinist?"

She frowned. "Haydn is the composer of the *divertimento* they just played."

"Who knew," Slater said, and looked back to the performers.

They launched into another piece, similarly up-tempo, and then a third, before finally taking a bow. Slater clapped along with everyone else, relieved it was over. It was easy to watch Cash performing—who could be bored watching such an attractive man doing something so passionately? But the music, even though it was light and accessible, wasn't especially compelling.

The three of them left the stage, and the crowd started to thin out. Slater took his cup and sat at a newly free table by the window, keeping an eye on the room. Eventually Cash appeared, still wearing his bow tie and carrying a backpack—the same bulky gray one his twin had been wearing on his retail excursion—and dropped into the seat across from him.

"When you said you had to be here," Slater said, "I thought you might be a barista. I didn't expect to see you working a flute."

"It's just for fun," he said. "I'm not getting paid."

"You should be. You look like you know what you're doing."

Cash watched him for a moment, his face relaxed, content. Slater knew that feeling behind that expression—the calm that comes after completing a stressful task.

"What did you think of the music?" Cash asked.

"You have to love Haydn," Slater said, swirling the dregs of coffee in his cup.

Cash's eyebrows shot up. "You recognized the piece."

"Is that so surprising?" Slater demanded.

"Well, you don't really look like a classical music guy," he said, his face reddening. "I realize that's stupid and judgmental—I don't know you."

Slater chuckled. "I don't actually know Haydn. Someone told me what it was."

"So you're just messing with me."

"I enjoyed watching you play," Slater said. "Are you a professional musician?"

He shook his head. "I can't afford to be. Music doesn't pay very well."

"I dig the bow tie."

"Maybe I'll let you take it off me," Cash said, meeting his eye. "I don't usually sleep with strangers, but you were pretty full-on flirty yesterday."

"I thought that was the point of meeting in a

coffeehouse. I watch you do your thing; we make some chitchat—lo! I'm not a stranger anymore."

"I guess that's partly true," he said, holding his gaze.

"We can take it slow, if you're nervous," Slater said gently.

Cash frowned. "I'm not a greenhorn. It's just that I usually only sleep with guys I've been out with once or twice."

"Sounds time-consuming, and boring, and sad," Slater said.

"It sounds like you have a bias against dating," Cash said, studying him. "Have you ever had a boyfriend, or a serious relationship?"

"Sure. I've got an ex that I still talk to."

"So you know there's value in the part of it that isn't just about sex."

"I wouldn't say that. He's an idiot. When he dumped me I almost broke in half."

Cash winced. "Ouch."

"What about Cash?" Slater said. "What's your relationship history?"

"Nothing as painful as that, I'd say."

"You never moved in with a guy," Slater said, "or stole his car when he pissed you off?"

"No," he said, and laughed. "Listen, this necktie is getting itchy. You said you lived in Westlake."

Slater sat up, shoving his cup aside. "Let's go. Are you riding with me?"

"I'm on my motorbike."

"You can park in my garage," Slater said, and told him how to find it.

———◆———

When Slater pulled into the alley, Cash was already there, helmet on, straddling his bike on the gritty broken asphalt a few doors down from Slater's garage, his white shirt and tie visible under his open jacket. Slater flicked his headlights as he pulled past him, pausing as the heavy shutter rolled up. Cash pulled in beside him and killed the engine, pulling off his helmet as Slater climbed out of the Thunderbird.

"Sweet ride," Cash said.

"Thanks," Slater said, waiting for the door to roll down.

"I can't believe you have a private garage in this crazy crowded neighborhood."

"It's a big part of why I live here."

"Is that a hedge trimmer?" Cash asked, looking over the gear hanging on the wall rack. "And a chain saw. Are you a gardener?"

"Gardening is like music," Slater said, unlocking the door to the stairs. "I enjoy it, but it doesn't pay very well."

Cash took off his jacket and threw it on the seat of his bike, then pulled his backpack on again, and followed Slater into the stairwell.

"I probably should have warned you," Slater said, glancing back at him, "my place isn't glamorous."

"I'm not worried about that," Cash said.

Slater unlocked his front door and held it open for Cash as he stepped inside.

Looking around, his expression shifted. "Whoa—you weren't kidding." Cash set his backpack on the kitchen counter. "Why do you live here?"

"It's got a great garage," Slater said, folding his arms.

Cash turned and met his gaze. "Did I mention my necktie was getting uncomfortable?"

Slater stepped closer, pulling on the ends to undo the knot, then unbuttoned his collar.

"Better?" he asked.

"You're so hot," Cash said, and took Slater's hand, pressing it to his cheek, turning his head into it and closing his eyes.

"So what are you into?" Slater asked, focusing on the soft warmth of his skin.

"You mean sex-wise?" he said, meeting his eye. "Anything, I guess."

"I'm not buying that," Slater said, pulling his hand away. "That's the problem with getting to know someone before you sleep with them. All the other stuff starts clouding the issue."

"What are you talking about?"

"Most people know exactly what they want. The issue is being able to ask for it."

Cash hesitated. "What if it's kind of crazy?"

"It's more fun when it's crazy, don't you think? I'm not going to judge you. I just want to aim for the maximum level of enjoyment."

He shifted on his feet, his expression turning serious. "So I should be completely honest."

"That would be ideal," Slater said, suppressing his impatience.

"Well, I guess I'd have to say that what I need is a firm hand."

"Oh, yeah? The rough stuff?"

He nodded solemnly. "I've been bad, Slater. Very bad."

That wasn't even remotely crazy, Slater thought, but he didn't say that. Instead he said, "I can work with that," and leaned in to kiss him. Cash's mouth was hot, intense, and tasted like coffee. He was good at this. Slater felt his cock swelling in his jeans. Pulling away, Slater slapped him, and Cash stepped back, eyes wide, touching his cheek with his hand.

"What?" Slater asked, his eyes narrowing. "Am I missing something?"

"No, no," he said quickly. "It just happened so fast. I thought it might take a bit more work to get there."

"Like waiting until the third date?" he

demanded, and looked pointedly at his pants. "Your cock has a different agenda."

"Right." He nodded. "It's totally hot. Just—don't be too rough."

Slater put his hands on his hips. "If you've been misbehaving, I'm going to need to set you straight, son."

"I get that," Cash said, breathing heavily now. He stepped closer, kissing Slater again.

After he leaned into it for a moment, Slater broke away and dropped to a crouch, grabbing him around the thighs, throwing him over his shoulder, and taking hold of his wrist on the other side. Cash yelped in surprise, but went with it. The firefighter's carry, they used to call it in wrestling. Doris had steered him into the sport in middle school, probably because she thought it would be an outlet for his aggression.

Carrying him into the bedroom, Slater rolled him onto the futon.

Cash looked up at him, exhilarated and laughing. "You're good at this."

"Take your shirt off," Slater snapped, and watched him undress.

Climbing on top of him, Slater pinned his wrists above his head, kissing him roughly.

"I didn't mean to do it, I swear," Cash said when Slater pulled away, breathing hard, his face red.

"You should have thought of that sooner," Slater said, and slapped his face. He watched him to gauge his reaction, not wanting to push him too far. But his eyes were bright—this is what he'd asked for. Slater started unbuttoning his own shirt, and Cash reached up, grasping his arms. Slater shrugged him off and slapped him again, then stood up and unbuckled his belt, sliding off his jeans.

"What are you going to do?" Cash asked, propped on his elbows, watching him.

"I'm going to fuck you and teach you a lesson." Climbing back on the bed, he added, "if that works for you."

"I think it's the only way I'll learn," Cash said gravely.

Slater paused to dig a condom and lube out of the bedside drawer, then pushed Cash onto his side, slapping his butt. Working his way in first with his fingers, eventually Slater penetrated him, then grabbed his cock, pumping it as he thrust deeper, relishing the sweaty intensity and building speed. Finally Slater came, pushing hard into him. Shifting focus to Cash, he wrapped an arm around his chest and stroked his cock until he arched his back and came.

Slater flopped onto his back, catching his breath. Cash rolled next to him, and Slater put his arm under his neck, pulling him close. It was too hot for prolonged contact, but he could stand it for a little while.

"I love the way you manhandled me," Cash said finally. "You're very intuitive."

Slater chuckled, folding his arm over his eyes.

"Have you got a towel?"

"In the bathroom," Slater said, and quietly got up as Cash left, waiting to hear the bathroom door close. He went quickly into the kitchen and clicked the light on, pulling open Cash's back-pack. The bulky shape inside, he saw, was a hard black case with metal latches. Flipping it open, he found the flute, in two pieces now. There was a laptop in the next pocket, but there wasn't time to mess with that. Behind it was a sheaf of loose paper—sheet music, he saw when he pulled it out, the notes written in pencil on a printed tem-plate. This wasn't what he'd been playing from in the coffeehouse; that had been a bound booklet.

Stepping back into the bedroom, he grabbed his phone. The water was still running as he took a photo of the top sheet of the music, but then the sound stopped. Slater shuffled the paper back into the bag and pulled the drawstring, flicking the light off as he stepped into the bedroom, just as the bathroom door opened.

When Cash entered, naked and flaccid, Slater paused to admire his body. He looked completely relaxed.

"I have to run down to my car," Slater said, pulling on his jeans. "I just remembered I left a bag of takeout in it. I don't want my car to smell like tacos."

"Based on your elegant apartment, I'm surprised you'd be worried about something like that," Cash said.

Slater grinned, pulling on his T-shirt, and walked out. There was nothing incriminating to find in his place, nothing to steal, he thought, trotting down the stairs, even if Cash started snooping. He always made certain of that, letting guys come here.

In the garage he unlocked the cabinet that sat just past the nose of the Thunderbird. It looked like a regular storage cupboard but it was heavily armored, more like a safe. Shovels, rakes, and a string trimmer hung openly on the garage walls, but more sensitive stuff, his surveillance gear, was kept in here.

One of the trackers in the arsenal he'd acquired from the Russians was designed to be slipped into a suitcase or a bag—like the backpack Cash had left in the kitchen. It was shaped like a clip-on bicycle taillight and had a sporting goods logo on it. The red LED even lit up if someone flipped on the power switch. Slater activated the tracker with the real switch, recessed and almost invisible, and the LED flashed twice, meaning it was active. The batteries wouldn't last as long as the heavy one in the beckoning cat camera he'd picked up today, but he might be able to learn something about Cash's movements.

When he went back upstairs, his kitchen was dimly lit by ambient light from the bedroom doorway, and he paused briefly to slip the tracker into an empty side pocket of the backpack. In the bedroom he stripped off his clothes again as Cash watched, a contented grin on his face.

"Where are the tacos?"

"They were cold and mushy," Slater said. "I threw them away."

Lying down with him, Slater put his arm around his neck again and kissed his hair. They stayed that way for a while, enjoying the connection.

"So what do you do?" Slater asked him eventually, shifting onto his side.

"My brother and I run a printing business. We make greeting cards, postcards, things like that."

"Like the stuff at the drugstore?"

"Those are mass-produced," Cash said, running his hand over Slater's belly. "Our product is more artisanal. Small batches, unique pieces."

"So you sell them at art galleries?"

"And funky little indie shops."

"Your brother's younger or older?"

"A little older," Cash said, pulling his hand away, his tone guarded now.

"Is he as hot as you?"

Cash chuckled. "Not quite."

"What's his name?"

"Why all the questions?"

"Just curious," Slater said casually.

"So what do you do?"

"Research."

"Not at a university, I'm thinking," Cash said.

"I track down deadbeats."

"What do you do with them when you find them?"

"Whatever needs to be done."

Cash shifted position to face him. "I could see you doing that. You can be intimidating."

"Only when I have to be."

"I should hire you to come with me on an errand tomorrow."

Slater glanced at him. He was being serious. Normally he'd say "I don't play the heavy," but this wasn't a regular client.

"What kind of errand needs a bodyguard?" Slater asked.

"I'm buying something. Don't ask me what. It's not anything illegal. I just don't trust the seller."

"So it's not illegal," Slater said, "but I can't ask

you what it is. In my business we call that a red flag."

"OK, so maybe it's slightly illegal," Cash admitted, "but it's not dangerous. No drugs or guns."

"It's not dangerous, but the seller might be. Is this person armed? I don't do weapons."

"He's not that guy. Not at all."

"So he's not a gangbanger, and not working for a drug cartel?"

"Not even close."

Slater studied his face, and tried to discern whether there was deception in it. With anyone else he'd insist on full disclosure up front before even considering a job like this, but he couldn't pass up the opportunity to see what Cash was up to.

"Sure, I'll go with you."

"Excellent," Cash said. "We'll go in the morning. How much do you charge for an hour's work?"

"If it's just an hour playing the heavy, with no prep time, three hundred. Cash up front. I'll drive."

"Where we're going, it'll be easier to take my motorcycle," Cash said.

Slater sighed. It felt wrong in so many ways, with all the unknowns, and significant elements like transportation out of his control.

"Do you have any food?" Cash said, sitting up.

"I was thinking those tacos sounded good."

"Peanut butter. There might be a Pop-Tart left. I guess you could get something delivered."

Cash scoffed. "No offense, but I can't stay here."

"I thought you had to be out of your place."

"I've got some other stuff to do," he said, rising.

Slater watched him get dressed, then walked him to the door, handing him the backpack.

"Until tomorrow, sweet prince," Cash said, and headed for the stairs.

It was too warm and sweaty to get dressed again. Slater pulled the fifth of bourbon out of the cupboard and took a pull from the bottle, then filled a tumbler and dropped in an ice cube. Grabbing his phone, he stretched out in the recliner, feeling the world already calming down as the golden leveler sank in.

The photo he'd taken of Cash's sheet music was legible, he found, zooming in on it. Too bad he couldn't read it. And Max had texted earlier:

Made the delivery to 402. No answer. Hanging out at 302 to hear the ghosts.

A while later, Max had texted again:

Cash just took in the package, when he let a woman into 402.

Slater dialed his number.

"I'm pretty sure that twin's name is Logan," he said, when Max answered. "Cash just climbed out of my bed."

"And you call me a mack daddy," Max said.

"I think I kind of went on a date with him first—I watched him play the flute in a coffeehouse. He said he had to be out of his place tonight."

"I bet I know why—I watched the other guy's date arrive. She looked totally hoochie."

"So it's hookup night for both of them. Isn't it weird that they're identical, but one's straight and one's gay?"

"Maybe Cash is only gay for Slater."

Slater chuckled. "Flattering, but far-fetched," he said, and told him about following Logan on his retail outing, and the plan he'd made with Cash for tomorrow.

"It's great that you're getting close to him," Max said, "but if you're bodyguarding, you really should have a piece."

"I know it's risky to go unarmed, but I can't pack a heater."

"Just try to keep your wits about you."

"So what did you mean," Slater asked, "when you said Logan's visitor was hoochie?"

"Did you watch the video?" Max demanded.

"I was busy."

"Watch the video," he said, "and see for your-self."

After he ended the call, Slater sipped at his bourbon, then pulled up the recordings from the Camellia building. Watching the video clips was like taking snippets of reality and trying to piece them together into a narrative. In the first one, Max arrived at 302, carrying the box with the cat camera in it and his duffel bag, and stepped inside. In the next clip he came out again, wearing the delivery uniform now and carrying only the cardboard box. The next video showed him knocking at 402, waiting for a few seconds, and then setting down the box and walking away. Next Max went back into 302, and then, a while later, a woman arrived at 402. Max was right—she was dressed for Saturday-night clubbing, not for the office, not for a weeknight at home with a friend. Her hair was ratted up, and she wore a skimpy tight cocktail dress, not carrying a hand-bag. Where were her keys and her money?

Slater wondered fleetingly if that's what he meant to Cash, the equivalent of his brother's no-strings paid date. But he'd invited Slater to watch him perform at the coffeehouse. Maybe there was more to it.

Pulling up the tracking app, the device he'd slipped into Cash's backpack was functioning cor-rectly, reporting its position, displayed as a green dot on a map. Checking the log, he'd stopped after he left Slater's apartment, for six minutes, just a few blocks away. When Slater zoomed in, he saw that it was a convenience store. Maybe Cash had gotten his tacos after all. Now he was southbound on the 5, and the marker under the map said "112 km/h." Slater knew enough about metric to know that was fast, but he wasn't going to watch. After all, he was going to see him tomorrow—they had a date.

Getting up to refill the tumbler, Slater took a sip and stretched out again, then put on a podcast, *Sasquatch Search*. It wasn't something he'd do himself, pursuing the massive cryptid in the boreal forest, but with his eyes closed, listening to the calm and methodical narrator, it pulled him out of this place for a while, away from this gritty city. Following the questers deep into the woods, he sank into the wilderness, the darkness of his own mind.

ELEVEN

A text from Cash woke him in the morning, and he checked the clock before he read it, glad that it was still early.

Ready in 30?

Slater texted back that Cash should pick him up at an intersection near his office. He needed to stop there first—no way was he going to pack a heater, as Max had suggested, but he could easily wear a wire.

Climbing out of bed, he washed up and got dressed, pulling on his faux leather jacket. It was too hot out for it, really, but it seemed appropriate if he was going to be on a motorcycle. The drive to the office was quick, and the building was humming with activity at this hour, porters with rolls of fabric and garments slung over their shoulders coming and going, but he found his own office empty and dark.

From the safe he pulled out the wireless mike he used sometimes in collecting evidence, and spent a minute pairing it to his phone, then attached it under his shirt collar. It would stay out of sight, but it was positioned to pick up any conversations he had. It didn't make sense to take his satchel, but he pulled a pair of black latex gloves out of it, just in case, folding them into his hip pocket.

A message buzzed his phone, from Cash:

Here. Where you at?

Slater locked the safe again and headed down to the street. Stopped at the end of the block in the red zone was a motorcycle, straddled by a black-jacketed rider—Cash. He was wearing his helmet, but Slater recognized the backpack. Motorcycles weren't a topic he knew anything about, but this one looked powerful and sleek, the design swept forward to imply speed. As Slater approached, Cash flipped up his visor.

"I've got your dough," he said, and dug in his pocket, pulling out a wad of tens and twenties.

Slater didn't count it, shoving it into his jeans, and Cash handed him the other helmet.

"Riding on the back won't be too emasculating for you?" Cash asked.

"Just don't crash," Slater said, and pulled on the helmet.

Climbing on behind him, he found the back footrests, then pressed his knees against Cash's hips and wrapped his arms around his belly. With that, Cash started the engine and pulled out, accelerating rapidly. Slater leaned into him, tightening his grip. The feeling of holding onto the guy, of not being in control, was exhilarating, like a living amusement park ride. He hated not being the driver, but letting go of that and just experiencing the ride was a rush.

Cash headed east, through the Arts District, then south. On two wheels he knew what he was doing, maneuvering between cars stopped at red lights and then accelerating past them, fast but not crazy.

They rode deeper into the industrial wasteland south of the rail yards, and eventually Cash slowed in front of a fenced lot fronting a windowless two-story structure. The heavy gate was rolled open, and Cash pulled through it, parking the bike in front of the loading dock, its steel shutter rolled closed.

Slater climbed off and pulled off his helmet. There were no cameras out here, which seemed unusual for a commercial site, and no signage naming the occupant, but the building was marked as an artists' space—the hazardous-chemical diamond sign, posted on so many industrial buildings, bore an A instead of the usual numbers that indicated the degree of danger inside. Why was Cash afraid to meet an artist? They were usually pretty innocuous compared to bangers and people like Svetlana and her crew.

Cash pulled off his helmet and took Slater's, attaching them to the bike with a cable and a padlock.

"How many people are we meeting?" Slater asked, watching him work.

"Just one, I think," Cash said, and straightened up.

Fronting the building, between the loading dock and the front door, was a rosebush, looking lush despite the small square of dirt it had to grow in and the lack of any other greenery. Slater didn't know the cultivar, but it was laden with a riot of showy pink grapefruit-size blooms.

"Are those peonies?" Cash said, noticing him studying it as he stepped to the door and pressed the bell.

"I know what peonies are, but they don't grow west of the Rockies," Slater said, eyeing him. "I thought you were an Angeleno. Where are your really from?"

"Illinois," he said simply. "Is it too warm here for peonies?"

"That, and the soil is too alkaline."

"Where are you from?" Cash said, frowning.

"Lifelong Angeleno, baby."

"I mean, how do you know that? I thought you were just a thug."

Slater sighed, struggling to suppress the urge to punch him in the face. "You saw my yard tools. I did horticulture in college."

The intercom crackled to life, with a voice unintelligible under the static.

"It's me," Cash said loudly. "Open up."

The door lock buzzed, and Cash pulled it open, stepping inside. A huge old industrial elevator sat facing the loading dock, its wooden gate half open, but Cash headed up the adjacent stairs.

"Hang back," Cash said quietly, "and don't say anything."

As they climbed up, Slater eyed the security camera mounted in the stairwell. Whatever was going to happen next, somebody had a clear record of their faces.

The room upstairs was a workshop, with time-worn wooden floors and bright daylight flooding in a pair of skylights. It looked like Svetlana's space, in terms of the clutter, but instead of electronics, everything here was metal, raw and polished, with several sprawling sculptures, looping tubular elements welded together. One of them was some kind of machine, rather than a piece of art, he realized, with a frame like a 3-D printer, but bigger. Maybe an automated lathe. An arc welder sat on the floor at one side. Was this place even ventilated?

Slater took it in for a moment, standing back from the broad work table as Cash approached it. The studio's lone occupant rose from a stool on the other side and walked around. The guy was scruffy, with an untended beard, his hair tied behind his head, and wore grease-stained coveralls, hanging open and revealing his sweaty chest.

"The artist," Cash said jovially.

The guy jutted his chin at Slater. "Who's this?"

"A friend."

"What did you do to the roses downstairs?" Slater demanded, hands on his hips.

He frowned. "I never touched those. What's wrong with them?"

"They're thriving, and I want to know why."

"You'll have to talk to the landlord. It's nothing to do with me."

"You have something for me?" Cash said, gesturing impatiently.

"It's ready," the artist said, stepping back to his table. "Do you want to have a look?"

"Looking won't tell me anything. I have to try it out."

The artist returned with a brick-size burlap package, tied with sisal twine, and handed it to Cash, who pulled his backpack around and dropped it inside, then pulled out a thick envelope.

It was cash, Slater thought, watching closely as the artist took it and stepped back to open it.

The artist scowled. "Why so many tens?" he demanded.

"It's money," Cash said. "What's the problem?"

"This wasn't the deal," the guy snapped, his face contorted in a sneer, waggling the envelope and moving toward Cash.

Slater quickly stepped toward him, in front of Cash, and the artist threw a punch, a fast left. Slater hadn't been prepared for that, and he dodged it but couldn't get out of the way in time. The blow landed at his left eyebrow.

Punching back blindly, Slater caught the guy in the gut. The artist stumbled back a few steps, then lunged at him. This time Slater was ready, and used a full-force knockout blow, landing it under his chin, using the guy's momentum against him. His head snapped back, and he twisted sideways, slumping to the floor.

Slater stood over him, rubbing his eye. "Fucking idiot," he roared, even though the guy clearly wasn't hearing him. "Why do you make me hurt you?"

Cash came closer, looking down at the crumpled figure. "Did you kill him?" he asked, wrinkling his nose.

"I coldcocked him."

"What?"

"He's just unconscious." Slater slid the black latex gloves out of his back pocket and pulled them on, wriggling his fingers.

"What are those for?" Cash asked, his brow furrowing.

"Leaving as little evidence as possible." Slater stooped and checked the pulse in the artist's neck, then gently probed his jaw. "Nothing's broken. He'll be fine."

Pulling the guy's legs and shoulder, Slater shifted him onto his side, resting his head on his forearm.

"It looks like you're staging a crime scene," Cash said, and when Slater didn't answer, raised his voice. "What are you doing?"

"I'm not staging anything," he said, scowling up at him. "If I put him in the recovery position, he won't choke on his own vomit."

The envelope Cash had given him had fallen to the floor, spilling its contents. Slater stooped to scoop up the bills, riffling them back into their container. There were some twenties and a lot of sawbucks in the thick stack. Why had the artist been upset with this? Tucking the envelope under the guy's arm, Slater rose and eyed Cash. Now that the artist was incapacitated, was he going to take the money back? But Cash didn't budge, staring at the unmoving body, his brow furrowed.

"You're not used to things getting rough, I'd say," Slater said.

"There are other ways to deal with trouble," he said, finally looking away. "Let's go."

"There are no cameras here, but we were filmed coming up the stairs."

"He's not going to be reporting us to anyone," Cash said, "unless he wants to go to jail himself."

Slater took a last look around the workshop, then followed him to the stairs. "Aren't you going to look at what you bought?"

"I know what it is," Cash said grimly, and pushed out the front door.

After he unlocked the helmets, they both put them on, and Cash started the bike. They both looked to the street as a car pulled up in front of the driveway, completely blocking it. A stripped-down fleet Crown Vic, it was gray, and unmarked, but unmistakably from a law-enforcement motor pool.

"Are they here for you?" Slater asked.

"I'm not sure, but I can't afford to be searched. Get on." Cash flipped his visor down.

As Slater climbed on behind him and notched his boots onto the footrests, a thick guy with a

cop haircut stepped out of the Crown Vic, looking intently at them.

"Hang on a minute," the guy called to them,
but the moment Slater's arms had encircled Cash's
waist, he gunned it, heading straight toward the
car, at the last minute veering left onto the sidewalk and racing to the end of the block. At the
curb cut he rode onto the asphalt and roared up
the street.

Slater couldn't look back to see if they were
being pursued, but Cash had mirrors, and he
was driving like someone was after him—moving fast, barely slowing for a stop sign, then a
right turn. Slater leaned into him, feeling the
unopened burlap bundle inside Cash's backpack
against his belly, following his body as it moved
with the inertia and the high speed.

Getting onto a busy boulevard, Slater pulled
his knees in tight as Cash split the lanes of vehi-
cles that were already traveling at the speed limit,
zooming between them with just inches to spare.
The bike was too loud to hear whether there were
sirens behind them, but at least there was no sign
of a police helicopter, not yet.

If they got caught, he needed a plan. An
edited version of the truth was fairly reasonable:
he'd just met the guy a couple of days ago, just for
a hookup, and he'd gone along on an errand to
help him out. The only incriminating stuff Slater

had on him was the surveillance software on his phone, and Svetlana's engineers had planned for situations like this. All he had to do was enter a specific code on the lock screen, instead of the one that unlocked the phone, and everything related to surveillance would quickly be erased. He focused on the code now, pulling it to the front of his mind as Cash raced up Alameda and under the freeway—112112, six simple numbers to wipe all traces of anything illegal.

Cash turned left, fast, across a break in the traffic, gunning it to avoid getting hit by an oncoming truck. It never could have stopped in time, would have sent them hurtling through the air. There was no way to communicate with Cash now, but he hoped the guy had a plan. Slater fleetingly considered jumping off the bike when he was moving slow enough, but that would only endanger them both. Closing his eyes for a second, he tried to recapture the exhilaration he'd felt earlier, when Cash was riding fast without pursuers.

They were downtown again, not far from Slater's office. Headed west on Ninth, Cash blew through the intersection where it became a one-way street. Had he even noticed the oversize DO NOT ENTER signs? He must know, Slater decided, as he was riding perilously close to the parked cars on the left side of the street—but only for a block. Cash turned quickly into the driveway of a parking structure, the one next to the whole-sale clothing mart. Racing up the ramp, then up another level, Cash finally pulled the bike into a corner. Slater hopped off, and Cash rode into the narrow space in front of the last car on the aisle, an SUV that was parked nose-in.

It was clever, Slater realized, pulling off his helmet and setting it on the concrete floor beside the bike—unless someone walked around beside the car, the bike would be hidden from view. There were definitely sirens nearby, now that he could hear without the engine noise and the hel-met. Slater walked up the aisle behind the cars, not looking back at what Cash was doing, taking deep breaths and willing himself to calm down and walk leisurely.

At the corner he went into the stairwell and ran up a flight, taking the steps two at a time. On the higher level, he walked along the row of vehi-cles toward the elevators, pulling out his car keys and letting them dangle from his hand. The sirens had stopped, and he pulled out his phone when it rang, answering when he saw it was Cash.

"I shouldn't have parked inside that yard," Cash said.

"You got away—so far, at least—so don't sweat it," Slater said quietly, glancing around the parking lot as he walked. "Thanks for not ditch-ing me."

"You're a good passenger. You didn't slow me down at all. Listen, you need to play it cool right now."

"I know what I'm doing," Slater said, irritated. "Why are they after you?"

"I don't think it was about me. It was just the one cop, right, and I'm not even sure they were following us."

At that moment a marked patrol car turned the corner in front of him, cruising slowly. "I've got to go," Slater said, and ended the call.

The patrol car stopped beside him, and the uniformed cop behind the wheel rolled down his window and gave Slater the once-over. "Where did you come from?"

Slater stopped and pocketed his phone, turning his palm up to display his keys. "From my car," he said, and frowned. "This is a parking garage."

"You work here?" the cop asked.

"My factory is over in the Del Rio Building, but my line is repped upstairs at Kawada Couture. We make faux leather menswear." He held out the side of his jacket. "You should come up and check it out. Fourth floor. You'd look good in faux leather."

"Did you see a couple of people on a motorcycle?"

Slater furrowed his brow in concern. "I didn't. Are they in trouble?"

The cop looked away, taking his foot off the brake and rolling off.

"Not even 'Ciao'?" Slater called after him, gesturing with his keys.

Walking into the mart, he strolled in a loop past the showrooms, taking his time but acting like he had a destination, then went down a floor and did the same thing. There was no sign of any police in here, so he took the elevator down to the street and walked toward his office.

Safely away from the building, he pulled out his phone and dialed Cash. It went to voice mail.

"I hope you're doing well," Slater said guardedly. "Give me a call when you get a chance."

TWELVE

ax looked up when Slater stuck his head into his office.

"What happened to your eye?"

"Is it messed up?" Slater asked, dropping into the chair in front of his desk.

"It's red. You're going to have a shiner."

"Cash's vendor got belligerent, but I flattened him."

"Do tell," he said, raising his eyebrows, and as Slater related the morning's events, Max pulled a pair of dress socks out of his desk drawer, stuffed one inside the other, then slurped the dregs out of his plastic cup of soda. Pulling off the cover and ditching it and the straw in the wastebasket, he stretched the socks around the rim of the cup and inverted it, dumping the ice into them. After he tied a knot in the socks, he handed them to Slater.

"Are these clean?" Slater asked, wrinkling his nose but taking the makeshift ice pack.

"Of course they are. You think I'm an animal?"

"You keep clean clothes in the office?"

"You don't?" Max said, frowning.

Slater held the socks to his eye. The cold felt good, numbing his skin.

"So why didn't Cash unwrap the bundle he bought?" Max asked. "That seems odd."

"He said that looking at it wouldn't tell him anything. He had to try it, whatever that means."

"How much did he pay the guy?"

"It was a stack of small bills, maybe fifteen hundred or two grand." Slater pulled the clandestine mike out of his collar, suddenly remembering it was there, and set it on the desktop. "You can listen to it all go down, if you want."

Max chuckled. "No thanks. I'm just glad you didn't get popped. What agency was the guy from?"

"I couldn't tell—he was in plain clothes. The workshop has to be in Vernon or Maywood, so maybe he was a county cop? I'm not even sure he was after Cash. He showed up at the artist's place, so it seems like they were after him. Cash and I were just there at the wrong time."

"Vernon has their own cops, but Maywood uses county."

"Whoever he was," Slater said, "Cash did not want to get caught with whatever was in that bundle."

"So I slept at 302 last night, and heard the baby again," Max said, reclining in his chair. "There was more moaning too. The woman in the short skirt left 402 before that happened, like at two. June went out at seven dressed for work. Around ten I followed Logan, if that's his name. He didn't take the motorcycle this time—we walked."

Slater shook the water off his hand, repositioning the ice pack. "They're sharing it. My guy had the bike today. The same thing happened on Tuesday, when you tailed Logan on the bike and Cash took the bus."

"We didn't get far. Logan walked to Wilshire, got coffee, ate at a deli on the corner, then went back to 402."

"I know that deli. You have to try the mushroom soup. It'll blow your mind."

Max frowned. "OK. What about Cash last night?"

"He wanted to bottom for me."

"Christ, not that," Max said. "You're punchdrunk. I mean, where did he go? He hasn't come back to 402."

"The tracker," Slater said, sitting up. "I forgot." Maybe Max was right—he wasn't thinking clearly.

Once he'd set down the ice-filled socks, he dried his hands on his pants and pulled out his phone. The map in the tracking app showed the green dot was near where they'd parted, inside the building rather than the parking structure.

"He's still at the mart," Slater said. "Or at least his backpack is."

"I hope he lets things cool off before he goes back for the bike."

Slater looked back through the log. "When Cash left my place, he went to the OC. He spent the night in Newport. Doesn't that seem weird? Newport is super white."

"Some Asians live around there too," Max said. "But you're right, it's not for Latin kids. Maybe he has an OC boyfriend."

"He told me he's from Illinois, so maybe they're not tuned in to the local segregation yet. Listen, can you read music?"

"Not a chance, brother. Why?"

"Cash had some handwritten sheet music in his bag. I photographed it."

"Maybe that's what he was playing in the coffeehouse."

"That was Haydn," Slater said. "It was in a book."

Max's phone dinged, and he pulled it out to look at it. "Activity in 402."

He turned to his computer and pulled up

the video, and Slater leaned forward to watch. A woman in a delivery uniform walked into the frame, pushing a hand truck with a corrugated box on it, bound with yellow plastic straps. One of the twins—it had to be Logan—pulled open the door soon after she knocked, and scrawled with a stylus on the machine she held out for him.

"It must be valuable, if he had to sign for it," Slater said.

The box wasn't that big, but Logan used both hands to heave it up and haul it inside by the straps.

"Heavy too," Max said. "Interesting that he opened the door for her, but not for me yesterday."

Slater looked at his phone and checked the camera app. "He hasn't opened the box with the cat in it yet."

"Maybe he noticed the shipping label," Max said.

"Thanks for the ice," Slater said, rising from his chair.

Down the hall in the men's room, he dumped the ice in the sink and rinsed out Max's socks, splashing water on his face to wash off the high-fructose corn syrup residue. His eye didn't look too bad yet, just red around the orbit, but he knew it would eventually darken. Hopefully icing it had helped.

Back in the front office he spread Max's socks

out on the desk to dry, then went into his own office and got comfortable, swinging his boots up onto the desktop. Conrad was at his station, he saw, checking his phone, and he thumb-typed him a query:

Any info on a police incident today?

Looking at the tracking app, he found the address of the artist's workshop and added that before he sent the text. Cash's location had changed—he was on Olympic in Koreatown, he saw, heading west at vehicle speed. That seemed like a good sign—maybe he was on his way home.

The one person he could think of who knew about music was Doris's brother Dave. The guy had been a cantor, so he must know how to read it. He really didn't want to connect with him, but he sent a text anyway:

Can I drop by your office?

Dave's response came soon after:

It would be a delight to see my dear nephew.

Slater scowled at the smarminess, already regretting this. After he printed out the photo of the sheet music, he stuffed it in his satchel and rode the elevator down to the street, walking across to his car.

Live Oak College was way out in the Valley, and cruising up the 101, Slater started feeling resentful at the sheer distance. The guard at the gate waved him into a parking structure that he had to pay to use, compounding his irritation. Climbing out of the Thunderbird, he looked up Dave's office number in his contact list, and in a few minutes he'd found the right building. He knocked on the door and then tried the knob, and finding it unlocked, walked in.

Slater had never been here, and was surprised to see how roomy Dave's office was. Besides lots of books, he had a drum kit and an electronic keyboard set up in the space. Rising from behind his desk to greet Slater, Dave was wearing a tweed jacket and dark-red pants. Tall and dark-haired, he seemed lighter, more relaxed here than when he was droning on like a professor at Passover, when all people really wanted to do was eat.

Dave stepped around his desk and gave Slater an awkward hug.

"What's with the red pants?" Slater asked, looking him over pointedly, then digging into his satchel for the sheet music.

"What happened to your eye?" Dave said, peering at him.

"A work-related injury."

Dave nodded, frowning. "How's your mother?"

"How should I know? Did you lose her phone

number?" Slater handed him the paper. "I need you to tell me what this is."

Dave took the sheet and smiled. "It's music."

Slater scoffed, struggling to suppress his frustration. "I know that much. What kind of music?"

"I don't teach composition anymore, but it has always been one of my passions. Isn't it amazing that there's a way to commit sound to the page? We can look at something Schubert wrote down two hundred years ago, and have a direct emotional connection to him."

"Is this Schubert?"

"Not even close," Dave said, raising his eyebrows. "I'm just talking generally."

"Haydn, maybe?"

"It's not him either."

Slater wanted to hold back, but he just couldn't, and slapped Dave's face, hard, left and right, a rapid kovac. "What does it say?" he demanded.

Dave planted a hand on his chest and shoved him away, then grabbed his own cheek, massaging it, and snarled, "I should call your mother."

"I've caused her enough grief over the years, don't you think? Why make her any more miserable?"

Breathing rapidly, he said, "Maybe I'll call the campus police, then."

"Are you still sleeping with that twenty-year-old?" Slater demanded, hands on his hips. "I wonder if Aunt Abby knows all the lurid details."

Dave's eyes hardened. "You can be a real little prick sometimes."

"I know that, Dave," Slater said, forcing himself to speak calmly. "If you'd just tell me what's on that sheet, nobody needs to get hurt."

"Five thousand years of scholarship in your blood, and you spend your time smacking people around. You were always such a hothead. I can't believe all that shrink work never sunk in."

"The only reason you're not bleeding right now is all that shrink work. Uncle Dave, if you don't focus, I swear I'm going to punch you in the face."

Dave sighed and looked at the paper. "It's someone's composition. It's not annotated, but it looks like a ballad, or a pop song. It might be someone learning to read music, because it's written by hand. You can do this more easily with software these days."

"Is it for the flute?"

"You can play any piece on any instrument, but I wouldn't say this was written for the flute. Maybe for guitar."

"What does it sound like?"

Dave stepped over to the keyboard, mounted on a stand, and switched it on. Setting the sheet Slater had given him on the music stand, he played through it. It was slow, even plaintive.

"It sounds like *norteño* music," Slater said.

"Good ear. It's got a time signature that's consistent with *norteño*. Maybe that's what the composer was going for."

"Can you tell me anything about the composer?"

"This isn't especially sophisticated, but it's not a first try either," Dave said. "Maybe a second-year music student. I'd say the music is Latin in nature."

"Is it any good?"

Dave shrugged. "That's completely subjective."

Slater took the paper from the stand. "Thanks for your help," he said, and headed for the door.

"See you at Thanksgiving," Dave called after him.

It was a dead end, he thought, walking back to his car. All he'd learned was that Cash had a hobby, and that Dave was still a dick.

On the freeway, in the stop-and-go late-afternoon traffic in the Cahuenga Pass, Slater's phone rang.

"Can we talk?" Conrad said when he picked up.

"We're talking now, genius," Slater said.

"Spare me your bullshit. I'll be at my station for the next hour. Text me when you get here."

The line went dead, and Slater glanced at the

screen to make sure he'd actually done that—Conrad had hung up on him. This must be important.

Rampart was almost on the way downtown, and soon Slater was pulling up outside the low-slung building. Before he climbed out, he texted Conrad:

Out front.

It didn't take long for him to appear, busting his way out the front doors, wearing his ballistic vest—he must have been on patrol. The look on his face when he caught sight of Slater was serious, and dark.

"Looks like somebody managed to land a punch," Conrad said, his tone authoritative, pointing to Slater's eye. "How did that happen?"

Slater eyed him, trying to ascertain his mood. Usually Conrad was pretty laid-back, but today, it seemed, he was in cop mode.

"How is that any of your business?" Slater said.

"You know, I take a lot of shit from you," Conrad said. "And don't you dare bring up your lame-ass blackmail thing, or I swear I'll blacken your other eye."

"What's gotten into you?" Slater put his hands on his hips.

"I put up with it because I know you need my help, and I thought somehow I could protect you. My logic is, if I arm you with information, maybe you won't stumble into something worse." He scoffed. "Is that completely crazy?"

"I don't need your protection," Slater said carefully. His instinct was to blow up at the guy, maybe gut-punch him, even though taking on a cop in front of a police station was a fight he could never win, but he held back. It seemed smarter to let him vent.

"Doris worries about you too," Conrad said, still glaring at him. "She talked about doing an intervention to get you off the bottle."

"I knew it," Slater snapped.

"We decided against it, though. I know exactly how you'd react—you'd drive out to the desert and just disappear, go on a bender that you wouldn't come back from. And who would show up to put the guilt trip on you anyway? Me and Doris and three guys from your hookup-app history?"

"Nobody needs to be telling me what to do," Slater said, scowling. "What is going on with you today?"

"What have you gotten yourself into?"

"What are you talking about?" Slater demanded.

"That thing in Vernon was some kind of federal investigation," Conrad said, lowering his voice and glancing over his shoulder at the entrance to the station. "Were you there?"

"By what agency?"

"Who knows? There are a fuck-ton of them. For us, they channel everything through a liaison. We got a request to assist in the pursuit of a motorcycle downtown, but the incident originated at that address in Vernon."

"Did they catch the guy?" Slater asked.

"It was over by the time we got involved. They didn't even find the bike."

"What was the want?"

"That's not in the records. It just said that a line of inquiry in an investigation took them to that address. It wasn't a warrant search—the investigator went there alone, and you'd always go with a team to serve a warrant. Probably he just wanted to talk to somebody. And before you ask, federal stuff is off-limits, so don't ask me to dig into it. I can't."

"Not even the name of the agency?"

"No way." Conrad crossed his arms. "You know, the report said there were two people on the bike."

"Interesting," Slater said.

"Was one of them you?" he demanded. "I never heard you talk about riding."

"It's nothing to do with me," Slater said irritably. "It just came up in a case I'm working."

"What case? Insurance fraud?"

"I can't tell you that. Maybe when it's all over."

Conrad stood watching him for a moment. "Slater, are you OK?"

"You don't need to worry about me," he said. "And quit plotting against me with Doris."

"There's no plot, so just let go of that idea. You treat us both pretty badly, you know that?"

Slater looked away. "I know," he said quietly.

"So stop doing it," Conrad said emphatically. "And don't get involved in evading the police. It's not going to end well."

Slater met his eye. Long ago a shrink had tried to show him how to read people and give them what they needed, and Conrad definitely needed something from him right now. Maybe it was gratitude. It seemed pointless, but he said it anyway.

"Thank you for your help today," Slater said slowly, then turned and went back to his car.

As he climbed into the Thunderbird, he watched Conrad walk back into the building. That had been weird. Why was Conrad acting like such a hard-ass all of a sudden, and why did he pretend to give a damn about Slater? It made no sense.

Glancing at his phone, he saw that the cat camera had been activated. He'd look at that later, but more important was what Conrad had just said—Cash had managed to get away clean.

THIRTEEN

On his way to the office, his phone rang as he was crossing the 110 into downtown.

"How did it work out with those phone records?" Andy asked him when he picked up.

"They were extremely useful. You should be charging money for that kind of work."

"That's what you said last night too."

"I didn't talk to you last night," Slater said, frowning.

"It's not surprising that you don't remember. You were pretty tight when you called."

Slater felt his heart pounding, trying to remember. Had he really done that?

"Where are you right now?" Andy asked.

"Funny you should ask," Slater said. "I'm a

block from your place. I can probably see your window from the next stoplight."

"Seriously? You should drop by."

"No, man—I've got things to do." Slater braked for the red light. "What did I say to you last night?"

"I'll tell you when you come over. It's incredible karma that you're ... driving right past my house at the moment I phoned you. Are you going to deny such a blatant directive from the universe? That sounds like asking for trouble."

The turn lane was empty, Slater saw, and that was Andy's street. The light went green, and the car ahead of him started to move.

"I'll be there in a minute," Slater said, and swung the wheel, making the turn. Signs from the universe were bullshit, but he needed to talk to the guy.

There was room for him in the lot beside Andy's building, and the universe had even thrown in the cheap evening flat-rate parking. Slater paid the attendant, then walked into the lobby and went up in the elevator.

Andy was wearing boxer shorts and a sleeveless undershirt when he pulled open the door.

"You didn't have to get dressed up for me," Slater said, stepping inside.

"What happened to your ... eye?" Andy demanded.

"I had a small disagreement."

"I'm not surprised, if you go around punching people," Andy said, walking unevenly into the studio. "I'm not going to have sex with you right now, so just get that … out of your head. I've got work to do. I don't have time for your shenanigans."

"Hey," Slater said sharply. "You invited me over here. Quit being such a dick."

Andy turned back to him and grinned. "I'm just joking around. I'm glad you came. I don't have time to fuck you, though, that part is true." He waved to the pair of easy chairs near the window. "Sit down. Do you want a coffee?"

"I don't need anything," Slater said, and dropped into one of the chairs, watching Andy awkwardly maneuvering toward the other. "Why don't you sit with me?" he said.

Andy stopped, and raised an eyebrow. "That works."

Slater put his hands on his waist as he got near, guiding him onto his lap, then put his arm on his back. Andy felt warm, and he didn't hesitate to lean into Slater's body, wrapping an arm around his neck. His involuntary twitching seemed to soften as he settled in. Slater buried his nose in Andy's hair, inhaling the heady scent of his sweat.

"What did I say when I called you last night?" Slater said.

"You seriously don't remember?"

Slater sighed. "I wish I could."

"Just emotional drunk stuff. You said I should charge for the work I did. You also said I was hot. Something about my charming smile, and my sweet little caboose."

"Oh, god," Slater said, turning away.

"Do you drink every night?"

"That's none of your freaking business. I don't need you telling me what to do."

Andy put an unsteady hand on his cheek, pulling him back, leaning in to meet his lips. Slater got lost in it, exploring his mouth, strong and warm and intense.

Eventually pulling away, Andy said, "You seem defensive about it."

"I saw my ex today. He said him and my mother were plotting an intervention."

"But you don't think you have a drinking problem."

Slater scowled. "Of course not."

"See, if you'd never considered it yourself, you wouldn't react that way. What you're doing is called denial."

"What, you're a psychiatrist now?"

Andy chuckled and rubbed Slater's chest with his palm. "When you have a disability like mine, you see a lot of medical people, and get great access to drugs. Chemistry is the answer to every problem. A few complaints about joint pain and tight muscles, and they showered me with Vicodin and benzos."

"So you're a junkie."

"Recovering," Andy said. "Three years clean. And I'm not telling you … what to do."

He kissed Slater's neck, nibbling and moving toward his ear, and Slater closed his eyes, massaging Andy's thigh, enjoying the proximity.

"So when is the dreaded intervention?" Andy asked.

"They're not going to do it. They know it would blow up in their faces."

"Well, if you ever want to … talk about it, I'm a good listener. I'm better at that than I am at speaking, anyway."

Slater chuckled and ran a hand into his hair. "This is nice," he said, and kissed him again.

Finally Andy pulled back, and climbed off.

"You've kind of got me wound up," Slater said. "You're sure you don't want to do more?"

"Another time, Romeo. You should go."

Slater got up and kissed him good-bye, then headed out, riding the elevator down to the street.

He didn't really need to go to the office, he decided, and drove the opposite direction, toward his apartment. Darkness was encroaching as he pulled into the alley behind his building and waited for the garage door to roll up. As he climbed the stairs, the bruise around his eye finally started to ache. He kicked off his boots and stretched out in the recliner.

Conrad was smart to have put the kibosh on an intervention. It's not like Slater was a tweaker. He was in complete control of his booze intake—even now he was showing remarkable restraint, sitting here not drinking, when the golden elixir was waiting right there in the kitchen.

The cat camera, he remembered, and pulled out his phone. There was just one file from it in the app. The video started with a blurry swirling jumble, eventually settling on Cash's face, seen from below, frowning at the lens as he examined the figurine.

"What the fuck?" Cash said. "Did you order this?"

The image blurred with motion, and stabilized on Cash's face again. But it wasn't Cash, or maybe the first one wasn't—this was his double.

"Why would I order this?" he said, his intonation the same, wearing the same puzzled expression. "What a piece of shit."

As he flipped it over, the camera panned the wood floor, the empty box, the bubble wrap Max had bought.

"The delivery idiots left it at the wrong apartment," one of them said. "The label says it's for the freaks in 302."

The video caught a flash of his shirt, the ceiling, the floor, then fixed on brown cardboard, close up and perfectly still.

Before the recording ended, one of them spoke, his voice muffled: "They need to be packing up and moving on, not buying crap."

Slater sat back, thinking about it, then watched the clip again. Also on the camera app was a subsequent smoke-detector recording of Cash, or maybe Logan, leaving 402 with the resealed box, and then another clip, from a moment later, of him leaving the box in front of the door to 302, not pausing to knock, and stepping out of frame.

Checking on the tracker in Cash's backpack, its location had last been recorded an hour ago, at the Camellia building. Below the map was a message: "выключение." He had no idea what that meant, but the graphic along with it, an emoji face with x's for eyes and its tongue sticking out, was unequivocal: the tracker was dead.

Slater dialed Max's number, filling him in on what he'd learned from Conrad. Max had already seen the video from the cat figurine.

"That last comment," Max said. "Doesn't it sound like they're trying to push Mike and Jessica out?"

"Definitely," Slater said. "The question is, why?"

"Did you notice they were wearing the same shirt again?"

"I can't tell them apart. I'm starting to suspect that's the point."

"I'm going to be in that part of town tonight," Max said. "I'll swing by there and pick up your kitty."

"Thanks, man."

After he ended the call, Slater texted Cash:

Were you able to recover your wheels?

His response soon came:

It took a while, but yeah.

Slater thought for a minute before responding:

I saw your misbehavior today at close range. I think you need some discipline.

Cash's response was a smirking emoji, plus:

Not tonight, but soon.

On the kitchen counter behind him was an almost empty fifth of bourbon, and its unopened twin was in the cupboard, both ready for him. He could feel them, golden and constant, patiently waiting. But there was one more thing he had to do tonight.

Dialing Garik's number, he got a generic voicemail greeting.

"Can I see you tonight?" Slater asked the

machine. "You could come over to my place."

Getting out of the chair, he went to the bathroom and got a towel, then into the kitchen, steadfastly avoiding a glance at the bottle on the counter, and got some ice from the freezer, wrapping the towel around it. He was dozing in the recliner with the ice on his eye when Garik texted back:

I shall be there in an hour.

Slater grinned at that and set his alarm, dozing until it went off.

———◦———

It was completely dark out when he woke. He got up and hid his satchel behind the sofa, stowed the booze, and put on a tight white T-shirt, like the one Garik had admired last time.

Right on schedule, Garik knocked at the door.

"Have you been fighting?" Garik asked, frowning and stepping inside.

"It was just a minor incident."

"Did you put ice?"

Slater pulled him close, kissing him. The guy let him do it, but he was so passive, like a warm mannequin. Leading him to the bedroom, Slater got his clothes off, and then pulled off his own. Garik lay on his back, his hands flat on the bed, and Slater kissed him, running his hands over his body, then stroking his hard cock. Their mouths locked together, Slater increased the tempo until Garik was breathing heavily, close to climaxing, and then pulled his hand away.

"Tell me about your client—a guy named Logan," Slater said.

Garik gazed at him, panting, looking confused. "What?"

"Logan is buying something from Svetlana. What is it?"

"We can talk after," Garik said, and reached for his own cock.

Slater slapped his hand away. "Just tell me what Logan buys from her. Then we'll finish this."

"My loyalty is always going to be to my family," he said gravely.

"Svetlana said she doesn't care about Logan. She told me I could take him down if I needed to. On principle she just doesn't want to gossip about what she sells to him. But you can gossip, can't you?" He grabbed Garik's cock and squeezed, then pulled his hand away, spreading his fingers in the air.

Garik closed his eyes and groaned. "Paper. It's just paper."

"You can get paper anywhere. What kind of paper?"

"I don't know. Svetlana compartmentalizes information. She sells him boxes of paper—I don't know what it's for. The delivery to him is Friday."

"Tomorrow?" Slater asked.

"That's all I know."

Slater grabbed his cock and kissed him again, stroking him until he came. Grabbing himself, he put his other hand behind Garik's neck. If the guy wasn't going to participate, Slater was going to make him be present, at least. Smelling his hair, probing his mouth with his tongue, Slater finally came, then rolled onto his back.

Garik got up a minute later and went to the bathroom. With his arm over his eyes, Slater listened to the water go on and then off. Cash had said he and Logan were artisanal printers, so the fact that he was buying paper wasn't a surprise. But what kind of paper required him to go to a back-alley vendor like Svetlana?

When Garik came back, he started to get dressed. "I have to go," he said.

What a relief.

"There's somebody I want you to meet," Slater said. "He's a big guy—thick and beefy."

"You mean for dating?" Garik said, raising his eyebrows.

"I like you, Garik, but I don't need a boyfriend. Maybe you could talk to this guy. I think the sex would work out."

"What does he do for a job?"

"He drives a package delivery truck. His name is Matías."

Garik nodded. "I will meet him."

That was very good news, Slater thought, and walked him to the door, locking it behind him.

The bourbon was waiting, right where he'd left it, and he guzzled straight from the bottle, gasping at the intensity of it as it burned his palate and the back of his nose. Pouring a tumbler full and dropping the empty bottle into the trash, he stretched out on the sofa, taking a sip and then setting the glass on the carpet. He turned on the radio, playing house music at this hour, and started to sink into the rhythm.

Garik was a dud, he knew that now, and he wasn't going to sleep with him again unless he had to. Foisting him on Matías would obviate that obligation to the Russians.

No phone calls, he thought, opening his eyes, remembering what Andy had told him. The last thing he needed was to drunk-dial people and give idiot Conrad and Doris more ammunition. Just in case, he went into the bedroom and put his phone in the drawer in his bedside table.

Back on the sofa, he took another gulp from the tumbler and set it down again, letting the music carry him into unconsciousness.

FOURTEEN

is head didn't hurt too badly when he woke up. Not as bad as it sometimes got. From the angle of the light in the window, it was still early. He was in his own bed. Reaching for his phone on the bedside table, it was missing, and he sat up, looking for it on the floor. In the drawer, he remembered.

June had gone to work this morning, he saw on the camera app, and last night Max had dropped by 302. Wearing his black suit and a natty navy-blue tie, he stooped to pick up the cardboard box with the cat figurine inside, then walked back toward the stairs, glancing up at the camera in the smoke detector and grinning.

Dialing Max's number, he told him what Garik had said about Logan buying paper.

"They hardly ever go anywhere," Max said. "They must be running the business in that apartment."

"That fits with what Mike said—he complained about the noise up there."

"Could you offer Svetlana to make the delivery for her?"

"No way," Slater said. "I'm not supposed to know about it. I weaseled it out of Garik under duress. If I damage the relationship I have with her, we lose all our tech."

"Knowing her, you might lose more than that," Max said grimly. "Maybe I can piggyback on the paper delivery. I can hang out at 302 and wear your delivery uniform. If they open the door, I'll ask where the box with the kitty is. At least I might get a look inside."

"As long as you tread lightly. I'm going to try to hook up with Cash again. Now that we know they're trying to push Mike and Jessica out, maybe we can figure out why."

After he ended the call, he texted Cash:

I want to manhandle you. Are you around today?

Climbing out of bed, he opened the fridge, even though he knew there was nothing to eat, eventually settling on a spoonful of peanut butter and some olives. He should probably go to the market at some point. When his phone buzzed,

he went back to the bedroom to find a reply from
Cash:

> I have to work later, but if we're quick. I don't have
> my bike—what express bus stop on Wilshire is
> near you?

Logan must be using the motorcycle today,
he thought, and texted him the info.

After he put on a T-shirt and boxer shorts, he
pulled the sheets up on his futon, straightening
the blanket. It seemed like there'd been a lot of
guys in this bed over the last few days. He wished
Rosa was coming sooner to do the laundry and
change the sheets. In the kitchen, Slater made an
ice pack out of a towel, then stretched out in the
recliner. He was dozing when there was a knock
at the door.

Glancing at the boxer shorts, Cash grinned
when Slater let him in. "Have you been out of the
house yet?"

"I don't need to go anywhere," Slater said.
"You came to me."

Stepping in and dropping his backpack
beside the door, Cash gently put a hand on Slater's cheek, studying his bruised eye.

"I'm sorry that happened," Cash said. "I never
thought the artist would go ballistic."

"You knew that was a risk, though, or you
wouldn't have hired me." Eyeing him and realizing

the guy truly felt bad about it, he added, "I'm just glad he wasn't armed."

"He didn't have time to arm himself. You flattened him with one punch."

Slater chuckled, running his fingers through Cash's thick luxe hair.

Cash leaned into him, meeting his mouth. Slater felt himself getting hard and put his hands on Cash's waist, pulling him closer.

"I sense a Hispanic uprising," Cash said.

"You ride like a maniac," Slater said softly. "I get a woody just thinking about that."

"Did I really cause trouble?" Cash asked, dropping his chin and looking up at him.

"Lots of trouble. I think it's time you paid for your misbehavior."

Slater grabbed his wrist and twisted him around, pinning his arm behind him, then hustled him to the bedroom, pushing him inside. Cash stumbled but caught himself. Breathing hard, he turned to Slater and started to unbutton his pants.

"Hands off," Slater snapped, pushing his hands away, and sat on the edge of the bed, unzipping his fly and sliding his pants down, then taking Cash into his mouth. Cash groaned with the intensity of it, and eventually Slater pulled him onto the bed.

The guy had a great body, and once Slater had

his own shirt off, he spent a minute exploring it, running his hands over Cash's bare torso.

Somewhere in the main room his phone made a sharp *blip-blip* sound. That never happened. It was from the Russian software, and he knew it was urgent.

"Give me a second," Slater said, and got up, finding his phone on the floor beside the recliner. Taking it into the bathroom, he checked the message:

User Max C erased all software.

This was not good news. Svetlana's software sent it as a heads up to give Slater a chance to wipe his own incriminating evidence, or to get away when someone else on his account had been ensnared. He'd almost done it himself yesterday, typing in the erase code on the lock screen, and because they shared the apps, Max would have received this notification.

But Max had been the one to wipe his phone. Below the notice was a button labeled TAP FOR LOCATION. It brought up a map where Max had been when he'd done it—the Camellia building, right where he said he'd be today. It wasn't clear what unit he was in.

When he dialed Max's number, it went straight to voice mail. Slater thought about it for a minute. Max must have gone into 402. He knew now what he had to do.

Exiting the bathroom, he pulled his satchel from behind the sofa and took out a pair of black latex gloves, quickly pulling them on.

"Are you OK?" Cash called from the bedroom.

"Be right there," Slater said, and dug in his satchel for a tiny blister packet that he knew was in one of the side pouches. It contained a small dose of an opioid that he'd obtained from a guy as a trade for services. He wasn't sure what drug it was, but it was concentrated, the guy had promised, and just the right amount to knock someone out.

It didn't look like much, when he found it, just a tiny tablet. Carefully peeling the backing off the packet, he held the little white dot in his palm, under his middle finger.

Back in the bedroom, he found Cash with one arm under his head, still with a raging woody.

"You left me with the engine revving," he said. "What's with the gloves?"

"We're going to take the discipline up a notch," Slater said, and pulled the bottle of lube from the bedside drawer. Kneeling beside him, Slater put one hand on his throat, right under his jaw, and with the other reached between his legs, massaging a finger into him, then another, pushing the miniscule tablet inside. Cash had his eyes closed, breathing hard, enjoying the intensity of it.

At the end of the bed a muffled gong sounded, and Cash opened his eyes.

"Time out," he said, pulling Slater's hand from his throat and sitting up. "I need to check that."

Rolling onto his belly, he reached for his pants and pulled out his phone, briefly studying the screen.

"I have to go," Cash said, his demeanor shifting. He stood up, stepping into his pants, then dropping to tie his sneakers.

"Something wrong?" Slater asked, reclining on his elbows and watching him closely.

"Family emergency." He pulled on his shirt, quickly buttoning it.

Slater wondered why the drug hadn't had any impact. Maybe the lube was acting as a barrier, preventing it from being absorbed, or maybe the guy who'd traded it to him had ripped him off. But then Cash paused, and looked at him.

"I feel kind of funny," he said, and took a step, but stopped, unsteady. Turning to scowl at Slater with hazy eyes, he demanded, "What did you do?"

Slater stood up in time to catch him as he slumped, lowering him onto the bed. Cash was out cold. If Logan was holding Max, now Slater had something to trade.

Peeling off the latex gloves, careful not to get any lube on his skin and potentially drug himself, he quickly got dressed, then checked Cash's breathing. It was slow but regular. Cash wasn't a big guy; maybe the dose was too much. At least he could bring him back, hopefully, if he did stop breathing—the guy who'd given him the drug had included an autoinjector of an opioid blocker, the kind paramedics carried, which he kept in his satchel along with the tablet. Hopefully he wouldn't have to resort to that.

The opposite problem was that he might wake up too soon. Slater went to the kitchen junk drawer and dug around at the back, looking for the pair of handcuffs he kept there. Checking his key ring to make sure he had the right key for them, he noticed Cash's backpack on the floor by the front door. He snatched it up and fished his dead tracker out of the side pocket, then pulled it over his shoulders and slung his own satchel over it.

Back in the bedroom, he cuffed Cash's hands behind his back, made sure the guy was still breathing, then rolled him into the blanket he was lying on, lifting him in the firefighter's carry. It was awkward getting out the door, and he bumped Cash's sneakers on the wall, but he got the deadbolt locked, and headed for the stairs.

Before he could get there, the claustrophobic little elevator dinged and its door rumbled open. Slater never used it, as it was slow and ancient and rickety, but his neighbor Grace did, and she appeared now, wheeling her black shopping pushcart out into the hall, loaded with grocery bags. She had a scarf over her hair and wore a sweater, even though it was blistering hot these days.

Stopping in the hallway, startled at first, she smiled when she recognized Slater. "Looks like you've been busy," she said, eyeing the blanket.

"Hey, Grace—I'm kind of in a rush. This is heavy."

"Still alive, then, is he?" she said, and winked at him, pulling her cart against the wall so he could get past.

"Thanks," Slater said, hustling toward the stairs.

"Do you need dish soap?" she called after him. "Drop by later if you do. It was on sale. I bought four of them."

"I will," he said, trotting down the steps.

Slater was lucky, he knew, to have a neighbor like Grace. He'd helped her out before, no questions asked, and in return he knew she'd never rat on him. Even in a deposition, she'd just sit there, wide-eyed and innocent, and swear she'd only seen him with a bundle of laundry.

When he got into the garage he was panting from the effort of carrying the dead weight. For a second he considered putting Cash in the trunk, but then decided on the backseat. Pulling the door open and flipping the seat ahead, he pushed him in, feet first, as gently as he could. He was still breathing, he found, and the pulse in his neck felt good, if a little slow. Slater rolled him onto his side and loosened the blanket around his head.

From the wall rack with his gardening gear he pulled down a pair of goggles and the chain saw, shaking it to assess how much gas was sloshing around inside. The tank sounded half full—that should be enough. Loading it into the trunk of the Thunderbird with his satchel and Cash's backpack, he slapped the button to roll up the garage door and climbed in, taking a deep breath as he twisted the key in the ignition.

Taking Sixth Street toward the Miracle Mile, he didn't push it, driving cautiously despite his concern for Max, not knowing what the hell was going on. No way did he want to get stopped with an unconscious guy handcuffed in the backseat.

Holding his phone in his lap, he watched the recordings from the camera app as he drove. Time-stamped just before Max had wiped his phone, a woman in a delivery uniform pushed a hand truck up to the door of 402. She knocked and off-loaded the box, then when Logan opened the door, handed him the machine to sign. As she turned to leave, towing her cart, Max appeared, nodding to her and stepping up to the door. He was empty-handed, but his weapon was visible, bulging under his belt in the back of his shorts.

"I left a package here by mistake on Wednesday," Max said, one hand on the door as Logan dragged in the box.

"I get a lot of packages," Logan said. "It's probably here."

Max stepped inside, the door swung closed, and the video ended. Minutes later, he'd wiped his phone—and no one had left 402 since.

It was still early enough that when Slater turned onto the side street in front of the Camellia building, he found a spot almost directly in front of the entrance. Max's little green Courier pickup was parked a few vehicles ahead.

Leaning into the backseat, he found Cash was still out. It would get way too hot in here, a black car on a bright summer day, even with the windows open—he couldn't leave him.

Slater climbed out and opened the passenger door, flipping the seat ahead, and scanned the street. If anyone saw him, it would be obvious what he was carrying, despite the blanket. Even rheumy-eyed Grace had instantly figured it out. But he had to take the chance. Scanning the street, the only people visible were at the far end of the block. A car turned onto the street, and after it went by, Slater stooped and dragged Cash out, throwing him over his shoulder, still wrapped in the blanket, then closed the car door with his boot.

Hustling across the sidewalk, through the jasmine and the sword ferns, past the fountain and into the lobby, no one was in sight. The elevator was too risky, he decided, and headed up the stairs, grunting with the burden. The muscles in his legs were burning by the time he got to the third floor. His heart was pounding and he was gasping for breath. In front of Mike and Jessica's door, he scrabbled in his pants for the keys. Had he misplaced them?

"Damn it," he hissed, but no, they were here, tangled in his own keys, and he got the lock open, maneuvering his cargo inside and slamming the door behind him with his foot.

"Max," he called, just in case, but the apartment was empty and quiet.

He carried Cash down to the bedroom and dumped him on the bed, then stood with his hands on his knees, struggling to catch his breath, his body flooded with adrenaline. Max's suit was here, the familiar grid-pattern one, draped over the easy chair by the window. Once his breathing had slowed a little, he pulled the blanket off Cash, rolled him into the recovery position, and went back out to the front door, not bothering to lock it, then down the stairs.

The wild-haired guy who'd confronted him

and Max earlier in the week about losing Internet access was strolling in past the fountain as Slater was walking out. The guy nodded in acknowledgment as they passed, no hint of recognition in his eyes. *Thank you*, Slater thought. Thank you for not being here a few minutes ago when I had a body on my shoulder.

Opening the trunk of the Thunderbird, Slater heaved out the chain saw and his goggles. There was a pedestrian not far away, down the block, but he held the scuffed orange motor out of sight, close to his hip, the blade angled down along his leg as he crossed the sidewalk and hustled inside. Back in 302, he locked the door behind him as he went in, then pulled on his goggles. He stepped over to the beautiful polished-wood staircase, elegantly curving upward to the blank white ceiling. Sweeping with the tip of the chain saw, he pushed aside the books and photos, everything crashing to the floor, clearing a path upward.

Pulling hard on the starter cord, he got the saw running, loud and smoky in the enclosed space. Climbing up the first few steps, he braced his feet and engaged the blade, revving it to full power and slamming it into the drywall of the ceiling, pushing against the kickback to hold it straight.

Meant to cut through thick tree trunks and branches, the saw made quick work of the ceiling and the joists above it. He'd never followed through with his plan to inspect the ceiling for intrusion from above, but now it mostly felt like air space between a little lumber and plaster. The worst thing would be if there was a heavy sofa or something parked on top, but there didn't seem to be, and Slater had quickly cut enough of a hole in the floor to climb through. It was easy, as the stairs led right up, and he held his breath as he pushed through the cloud of plaster dust, chain saw first. He had to swat splintered floorboards aside, but then he was in, stepping into 402.

Max was sitting a few feet away, in the same place Mike and Jessica had their living room furniture, in a folding chair, hands behind his back, his bare knees at eye-level as Slater climbed through. Near the front door stood Cash—no, it was Logan—mouth gaping, rooted to the floor. Their eyes met for a moment, and then Logan sprinted toward the kitchen.

"Quick," Max shouted. "He's going for my weapon."

Slater dropped the chain saw, scrabbling over the broken wood, and went after him, tearing off his dusty goggles. Just as Logan reached for the ugly gleaming handgun, sitting on the counter with Max's phone, incongruously between the kitchen sink and a loaf of bread, Slater caught hold of his collar, yanking him backward. Logan's hand was on the weapon, but he didn't quite get hold of it, and it clattered to the floor.

Logan twisted around and clawed at his head, but Slater threw a quick dick-punch, and he stopped, crumpling in half. Wrapping an arm around his neck, Slater notched the guy's Adam's apple into the crook of his elbow and squeezed, cutting off the blood flow, careful not to compress the trachea. It was faster and more effective than cutting off his breathing, and Logan struggled and grabbed at him, but after a couple of involuntary spasms, he went limp.

Max cackled with joy, craning to see into the kitchen. "You put him to sleep?"

"Are you OK?" Slater called to him, grabbing the weapon and tucking it into the back of his belt, then dragging Logan into the living room, hands in his armpits, shuffling backward.

"I've been implementing that sangfroid thing you told me about," Max said. "Can you unhook me?"

"I need to tie him up before he comes to."

"The flex cuffs he used on me were in the second or third drawer."

Slater looked in the direction Max had nodded and stepped over to the full-size red tool cabinet, the kind mechanics used. In a drawer were several pairs of handcuff-style zip ties, and he took a pair, walking back to Logan, who was starting to stir. He zipped the plastic band onto one of Logan's wrists, then scanned the room, looking for something to tie him to.

The place looked more like a construction site than a residential apartment, with the walls broken open for a few feet up from the floor in several places. Slater dragged Logan over to one of the ragged holes in the plaster, where an ancient narrow-gauge pipe was exposed, running horizontally inside the wall.

Logan was blinking and groggy, coming back to consciousness. Slater heaved on the pipe with both hands. It didn't budge, not even a little, and Slater dragged Logan against the wall, propping him up, threading the zip cuffs behind the pipe and pulling them tight onto his other wrist.

Once he'd made sure the cuffs were secure, Slater rose, and took a breath, and looked around the room. Every wall had been broken open, exposing the slats under the plaster, the old pipes, and in places, newer electrical conduit. Black and red wires ran in a jumble from the holes along the baseboard. Aside from the mechanic's tool kit, there were corrugated boxes stacked amid plastic drums, two long tables laden with machinery, and an air mattress with a sleeping bag on it under the corner windows. The folding chair Max was tied to, along with a couple of matching ones and some barstools at the tables, were the only approximation of traditional furniture.

"What the hell are they doing in here?" Slater said, half to himself.

"Would you unhook me?" Max demanded. "You'll need a blade."

Slater went to the kitchen and found a paring knife, then crouched behind Max's chair and carefully cut one of the plastic bands. The cuffs were coiled around the frame of the chair, and they were too tight—Max's hands were an ugly shade of purple.

Max roared with the pain of regaining circulation, rising from the chair and wriggling his fingers, rubbing his wrists.

"Man, was I glad to see you," Max said, meeting his eye. He was wearing Matías's delivery uniform, and he paused to hike up the shorts before stooping to grab the plastic cuffs, examining them closely. "These are purpose-made to be used as handcuffs. That little fuck."

Slater swatted the plaster dust off his jeans and his shirt, and raked it out of his hair with his fingers, glancing at Logan. His eyes were open and he was blinking, but they were unfocused, and he hadn't said anything yet. Handing Max his weapon, he asked, "How did he disarm you?"

Max sighed and tucked the gun into the back of his waistband. "I let my guard down. When he let me in here, I was gawking around at the place, and he grabbed it out of my belt."

Looking around the room, Slater nodded. "I get it. This place is crazy."

Still working his hands, Max stepped over to where Slater had dropped the chain saw, peering down through the splintered gash in the floor. "I guess I should have got payment in advance from Jessica and Mike."

"Yo, fuck-face," Logan said, struggling with the plastic cuffs. "This is kidnapping. Let me go."

Slater and Max both turned to look at him.

"You're not in charge anymore, little man," Max said.

Logan frowned, eyeing Slater. "You're the guy Cash was bonking."

"How do you know that?" Slater demanded.

"Fuck you," he spat. "Let me go."

Slater sighed. "Two choices, Logan. You can answer some questions, or you can sit there and shut up."

Logan scoffed. "Are you two working together? It's still possible for you to avoid serious trouble. Just let me go—right now."

Max clicked his tongue and shook his head.

Logan looked to Slater. "Do you know this guy? He claimed he was looking for a package, but he broke into my home with a gun—I had to tie him up."

"One more word," Slater said, "and I'll tape

your mouth shut."

"I've got a better one for you," Logan said. "Untie me right now, and I won't call the cops."

Slater stepped over to the work table. "Why does it always have to be the hard way?" he muttered, and looking at Logan, demanded, "Why do you make me do this?" He'd noticed a roll of duct tape here earlier, and he picked it up now, moving toward Logan, peeling off a strip of it with a loud squawk.

"Are you fucking kidding me?" Logan shouted, as Slater crouched in front of him.

Logan whipped his head away, but Slater grabbed his neck, just under his jaw, pushing his head back. Holding him still enough to slap the tape over his mouth with his other hand, he pressed it on firmly.

"Thank you," Max said.

Slater watched Logan for a moment to make sure he could breathe, ignoring the murder in his eyes.

"It won't adhere for long," he said, tapping the spot over Logan's mouth. "He'll sweat it off." Rising, he turned back to Max. "What happened after he disarmed you?"

"He tied me to that chair and tried to get into my phone. I gave him the Russian erase code."

"I'm so glad you did that," Slater said. "It's why I came."

Max nodded. "After he saw that he was locked out of it, he made a lame-ass attempt at interrogating me, slapping me around like a nine-year-old would."

"Cash was the same," Slater said. "When I decked that artist, he almost fainted. These two are far from hard-boiled."

"Eventually he said his brother was on his way back. I'm not sure whether they were going to off me or leave me tied up while they fled. I guess they would have decided when Cash got here."

"I was with him when he got the message," Slater said. "He's downstairs."

"In your car?" Max said, frowning. "He's just waiting?"

Slater glanced at Logan. "Give me a hand," he said, and picked up the chain saw, then went to the front door. "We need the key to get out."

Wordlessly Max went over to Logan and squatted beside him, reaching into his pants pocket. Logan flailed and kicked at him, but Max slapped him hard across the face, then pinned Logan's thigh with his knees, finally rising with the key in hand.

Slater waited as Max went to the kitchen to retrieve his phone, then watched as he used the key to unlock the door. It was a complex piece, with multiple grooves and protrusions on four sides, definitely next to impossible to copy. Pulling open the door, Max waited for Slater to follow him out, then locked it again, pocketing the key.

Slater led the way down to 302 and opened the door.

"Good god," Max said, looking around. Books were scattered on the floor, chunks of plaster and splintered wood littered the staircase, and dust coated everything. The sickly sweet smell of two-stroke engine exhaust hung in the air.

"Cash is in here," Slater said quietly, setting down the chain saw and heading toward the hall-way. "He's knocked out. I'm not sure for how long."

Max followed him into the bedroom, looking over the unconscious twin. "He's wearing the same shirt as the one upstairs. What did you give him?"

"I'm not sure. Some kind of opioid."

"Should we carry him through the hole you made?"

"It would be easier to take him up the stairs in the hall," Slater said. "But then we risk being seen."

"Did you notice the Persian carpet in the living room? We can roll him up in that," Max said, and went back down the hall.

It was a good idea, Slater saw, assessing the carpet under the coffee table. It was the right size, and it was stiff, unlike the blanket. With two of them carrying the ends, it wouldn't look like a body.

Max hefted up the coffee table, setting it aside, and Slater rolled the carpet into a tube, lifting one end and waiting for Max to take the other. Carrying it to the bedroom, they set it beside Cash and rolled him into it.

"The little fucker is heavy," Max said, lifting the end with Cash's feet off the bed. "How did you get him up here?"

Lifting the other end with both hands, Slater led the way and opened the front door, and Max was able to close it again without dropping his end of the load. On the stairs they passed a woman on her way down, who smiled and asked, "Moving in?"

"Just delivering a carpet," Slater said, affecting his fake Spanish accent.

Glancing over his shoulder to make sure they were alone, Max set down his end and unlocked the door to 402, stepping inside. Slater didn't wait for him, dragging the carpet in and gingerly unrolling it as Max went to close the door. Seeing his unconscious brother appear, Logan screamed at them through his gag.

Slater put two fingers on Cash's neck to check his pulse, then looked at Logan. "He's fine."

"You should tie him up too," Max said. "Take your cuffs off and use a pair of theirs."

Slater dragged him to the wall opposite Logan, where another pipe was exposed under the plaster that had been broken away.

"What is that?" Max asked, watching Slater test the strength of the ancient rusty pipe by heaving on it. "That's an outside wall, and there's no plumbing."

"These old buildings had gas lines all over the place," Slater said, unlocking the metal cuffs on Cash and pocketing them. "Small-bore and running near the floor. Nobody uses gas heaters in every room anymore, so these days they're usually abandoned."

Max handed him a pair of the plastic zip cuffs, and Slater propped Cash against the wall, securing his hands to the pipe.

"Now what?" Max said.

Slater rose and waved at the room. "What the freaking hell are they doing in here?"

FIFTEEN

Max stepped toward the work table. "We should be able to figure out what this stuff does."

Slater followed him, looking over the machines.

"He told you they were in the printing business," Max said. "Doesn't this thing look like a paper cutter?" He pulled down a handle on the machine, exposing a blade that dropped evenly into a groove on the bed below.

"It's old-school, though," Slater said, examining the device. The mechanism was made of cast iron, and the bed was age-darkened wood.

A larger machine of similar vintage stood on the next table, with a big hand wheel at one side. Slater grabbed the knob and cranked the wheel, which lowered a flat plate toward the tabletop. He stopped before it made contact. There was no paper in the bed, but it was obvious what it was designed to do.

"This is a printing press," Slater said, and leaning over it, cranked the wheel in the opposite direction. The plate rose, exposing the metallic printing surface. Looking closely, he suddenly realized what it was: a negative engraving of the back of a ten-dollar bill.

"Look at these," Max called to him from farther down the table. He held up a pair of tens, then flipped them over, revealing the front to be blank.

"They're printing money in here," Slater said.

"Some of these are printed on both sides," Max said, digging through the paper. "So far I'm only seeing ten-spots."

Slater stepped over and examined one of the bills, feeling the paper between his fingers.

"They look real to me," Max said. "They feel right."

Set out on a strip of white fabric beside the machine were two other plates, slightly larger than a banknote. When he looked closer, they were engraved with the image of the front of the ten, complete with the fine cross-hatching on Hamilton's jacket, the waves in his hair.

"That's what Cash must have bought from

the artist—one of these engraved printing plates," Slater said. "His workshop was full of metal stuff."

"I can understand why he ran, then. You wouldn't want to get caught with that."

"The drums must be the inks," Slater said, looking around the room.

"You'd need solvents too," Max said, "and who knows what else. You're very lucky they weren't storing those on the floor where you came through with the chain saw."

"You're right," Slater said, glancing at the splintered hole. "I knew there might be furniture, but I figured I could cut through a sofa or an armoire. I guess I'm lucky I didn't get drenched in ink."

"Or go up in a fireball," Max said pointedly, "when some flammable chemical flooded down onto your chain-saw motor."

It had been rash, Slater saw that now, to cut through the floor. Still, Max was the one who'd let a twinkie half his size disarm him. But he didn't say that.

"So do we call the cops?" Slater said.

"That sounds messy," Max said, "and complicated. I know a guy who works with the feds, downtown on Fig. Federal enforcement of something or other. I'm not sure if his agency would handle this specifically, but printing your own money is definitely in Uncle Sam's wheelhouse.

He'll know who to send."

"You don't think he'll just tell you to call the local police?"

"Not when I tell him what we found here."

"I want to ask them some questions first," Slater said, looking at Cash, slumped against the wall.

"That one's not very cooperative," Max said, gesturing to Logan, "and your boyfriend is out cold."

"Cash will talk to me. I have an opioid blocker in my car. Let me go get it."

Slater went out and trotted down the stairs. As he was crossing the lobby, June came in, dressed for work. Lawyers must close up shop early on Friday. She smiled as she passed him, and he nodded, walking out to the street and opening the trunk of the Thunderbird. Pulling Cash's backpack onto his shoulders, he retrieved the autoinjector from his satchel.

Back upstairs, he dropped the backpack beside the tool cabinet and went over to Cash, kneeling beside him and unsheathing the device, then pressing it into the fleshy part of his outer thigh. It would work right through his pants, he knew, and he held it there until it beeped, meaning it had done its job. Cash didn't react, or even stir, but Logan shouted through the gag when Slater jabbed his brother.

"You should come and see this," Max called from the back of the apartment.

Slater rose and went into the hall. A few feet of wall had been ripped open directly across from the bedroom door, and inside the bedroom, three of the walls had ragged gashes in them too.

"Why did they rip this place apart?" Slater asked, stepping into the room.

A suitcase full of clothes was splayed open on the floor, and there was another air mattress with a rumpled sleeping bag on it. The most eye-catching thing in the room, though, was a briefcase full of cash—bundles of twenties, bound with rubber bands, packed tightly together.

"They've been busy," Slater said.

Max was kneeling at one of the holes in the wall. "Pull on the wire."

There were actually three wires woven together, Slater saw, crouching beside him, two coated and one bare. The red and black wires ran to a pro-looking audio component sitting in the middle of the floor, and the bare one was secured at the edge of the hole with a wood clamp. Together, all three disappeared downward in the narrow dark space. Pulling on them, hand over hand, they came up freely, but it felt like there was a weight at the end. In another few feet, the heavy object appeared: flat and black, open on one side—a speaker. Slater tapped the paper cone with the tip of his finger. The bare wire was anchored to the speaker's frame, and the other two were connected to its terminals.

"The ghost," Slater said.

"The wires run to that wall too, and that one."

"Speakers hanging inside the walls on all four sides. That must be how they made it sound like the voices were in the middle of Jessica and Mike's bedroom."

"It also explains why these clowns cut open the walls," Max said. "No way are they getting their damage deposit back."

Cash's voice came from the next room. "Why are we tied up?" he said, and then louder, "Help!"

Slater hustled back down the hall, eyeing Cash as he approached. That reversal drug was amazing—he looked totally lucid.

"Hey, Cash," he said. "How are you doing?"

"What did you do to me?" Cash demanded. "My head is killing me. How did we get here? Why did you tie us up?" Looking at Max as he entered, he added, "Why is there a delivery guy in our apartment?"

"You don't get to ask the questions right now," Slater said.

"Fuck you," he said, scowling in anger. "Let me go."

Slater crouched in front of him. "I had to drug you. You were out for a couple of hours, but you're through it now."

"You drugged me? We didn't drink anything."

"It was a booty bump."

"You fucking psycho."

"So who's the brains in this operation?" Slater said, ignoring his vitriol. "You or your brother?"

Cash kicked at him, but Slater grabbed his sneaker before it made contact, tossing his leg away. Moving closer, Slater slapped him hard on the cheek, then on the other side, a rapid kovac.

Across the room, Logan screamed through the duct tape.

"I really don't want to mess up that pretty face," Slater said, "but I will if you don't sing."

Cash glared at him, red-faced, hurt and hatred in his eyes.

"I know what you're doing," Slater said, "but why were you doing it here? This isn't an industrial space."

Cash closed his eyes for a moment, and turned away, taking a deep breath before he spoke. "It just sort of happened. We had the letter press here first, when we moved in. We talked about renting a commercial space, but we've worked in shops before, and people feel entitled to walk into those places. Your home is easier to keep private."

"Was the artist upset yesterday because you paid him with so many ten-dollar bills?"

Cash nodded. "He must have thought they

were bogus. He knows we only make tens."

"Were they fakes?"

Cash met his eye. "Some of them."

"You paid me with lots of tens too. Were those fakes?"

Looking away, he didn't answer.

"Why tens?"

"Stores don't check them like they do larger notes."

"Why is it only you on the lease?" Slater asked. "You both wear the same shirt, the same backpack, and downtown you used Logan's name. Svetlana knew you as Logan too."

His eyes grew wide. "You know Svetlana?"

"Answer the question."

Cash scowled. "What choice do I have? You've got me chained to the damn wall."

Slater gestured impatiently.

"It's a twin thing. We use just one identity for the printing business. One name on the lease, one motorcycle. As long as we don't go out together, and we wear the same clothes, it looks like there's just one of us. If things get too hot, we figured we could move on and use the other identity for a while."

Slater looked up at Max. "Questions?"

"Why were you harassing the people downstairs?" Max said.

Cash frowned. "We weren't harassing them.

We were subtly encouraging them to move out."

"Why?" Max demanded.

"They were a pain in the butt, always complaining to the manager about noise. We figured we could take over that unit, open those stairs, and do the quieter stuff down there."

"How did you know the stairs were there?" Slater said. "Up here it's just floorboards."

"*Was* just floorboards," Cash said, glancing at the splintered broken mess. "The building manager mentioned the original configuration, so one night we hung a camera down outside their window and got a look. Are you the one who broke through?"

"How did you generate the ghost noises?" Max said. "The baby, the woman crying."

"How did you know about that?" Cash said.

Slater snapped his fingers, looking him in the eye. "We're asking the questions, remember?"

"Logan can explain." Cash looked over at him. "Why did you gag him?" Looking at Slater and scowling, he added, "You get off on this, don't you—tying people up, smacking them around."

"We should probably take the tape off before we call in the G-men," Max said.

"Call who?" Cash said quickly. "Why would you call anyone? Let's just talk about this."

"Do you have a spray can of penetrating oil?" Slater asked.

Cash jutted his chin at the red toolbox. "In the cabinet. Bottom drawer."

Slater went over and found the can, and took a rag from the tabletop, then knelt beside Logan.

"It won't hurt if I use this to peel the tape off," he said. "Hold your breath while I'm spraying it." Lifting one edge of the tape, Slater said, "Deep breath," and waited for him to inhale, then spritzed the oil under the tape, massaging it in with his finger. Gradually he peeled it completely off, wiping the oil away with the rag.

"You fucking psycho," Logan spat, once Slater stood up.

"I was being nice," Slater said, frowning. "If I'd ripped it off like a bandage, you'd be bleeding right now."

"How did you make the baby ghost noises?" Max asked him.

"Fuck you, delivery man," Logan said, glaring at him.

"Just tell him, bro," Cash said. "Give them what they want, and we can talk about what we want. They're not cops, right? That means this is still negotiable."

Logan sighed, looking from him to Max. "The sound had to go through the wall, which blocks out all the higher frequencies. A regular speaker would sound muffled, but software can process the signal to compensate for the barrier.

We had to wear earplugs up here, because it was so damn loud, but downstairs they were hearing it in full-range high-definition audio."

Max looked at Slater. "What do you think?"

"It fits with everything we've seen," Slater said. "I guess I believe it."

"About the audio, or about everything?"

"All of it," Slater said.

"So why is the package delivery guy trying to bust up our operation?" Logan said, looking at Max.

"And why is he in cahoots with a two-bit hoodlum I picked up in a bar?" Cash added.

"Did you pick me up?" Slater asked, looking at him, hands on his hips. "Or did I pick you up? Look past your ego for half a minute, son."

"It's rich that you're calling him a hoodlum," Max said. "You're the one who got into a high-speed pursuit with the cops."

"I got away, though, didn't I," Cash said, glaring at him.

"Until now," Max said intently. He looked at Logan. "I can't get over how similar you two are."

"Listen," Logan said. "You're working for the freaks downstairs, correct? Maybe we can work something out. We'll stop bugging them, and patch up the floor. And since you're not cops, let us pay you to stay out of our business."

"With freshly printed bogus sawbucks?"

Slater said. "I don't think so."

"There's real money too," Cash said. "We're distributing our product all over the country, turning it into real cash."

"It's not just the money," Max said, waving his arm around at the room. "This is a disaster waiting to happen. All these chemicals could blow up and kill half the people in the building."

"So we made a mistake," Logan said. "Don't throw us to the wolves."

"I'm going to call my contact," Max said to Slater.

Slater held up a finger. "Let's think about the timing of that," he said, furrowing his brow. "Besides being frat-boy dicks to their neighbors, have they really hurt anyone?"

"You can't print your own money, Slater," he said emphatically. "They're undermining the almighty dollar."

"True," Slater admitted.

Max gestured at Logan. "Besides, that one smacked me in the face when he couldn't get into my phone."

"OK," Slater said, nodding. "But imagine you could look beyond your personal disagreement with him. Maybe we can adjust the sequence slightly."

"Explain," Max demanded, scowling at him.

"We're not going to take a payoff. But maybe

we could make them promise not to print any more money, and make that phone call to your friend a bit later."

"Why would you do that?" Max shouted, spreading his arms. "Why would you let them go?"

"They're so young," Slater said calmly. "It's not a violent crime, they don't have weapons here, and we both know they're not hardened criminals."

"Are you sure you're thinking clearly?" Max said, calmer now. "You're not just feeling sympathetic because you have an emotional connection to that one?"

"Maybe," Slater said. "But you have to admit that this feels like a first mistake. The feds will drop the hammer, and put them away for twenty years. You know they will, Max. Doesn't that seem excessive for what they did? We're going to report it either way, but we could at least give them a chance to run."

Max sighed, pressing his lips into a tight line. "How do we explain the hole in the floor?" he said finally.

"We were investigating the noise in 302," Slater said, "and came up to talk to the tenants in 402. We smelled chemicals, but there was no answer, and we couldn't get through the front door. We thought it might be urgent, so we used the chain saw, and found an empty print shop and the bogus sawbucks."

Max thought about that. "Why did we have a chain saw?"

"I had it in my car. I was going to cut back my mom's bougainvillea later. It goes nuts this time of year."

"How do you know these two won't go set up the same business somewhere else?"

Slater looked at Logan, then at Cash. They were smart to let this conversation play out, not chiming in.

"Fellas?" Slater said. "What do you say?"

"We won't, man," Cash said. "Not a chance. We're on the straight and narrow from here on in."

"We've learned our lesson, sir," Logan added quickly. "No more forgery for us."

"Just stop," Max said, scowling. "You're both overselling it." He looked at Slater. "So there's no guarantee that they won't keep doing it, but you want to let them go anyway."

"Only if you're down with that," Slater said, shrugging. "For you and me, it means a slight adjustment in the order of events, that's all. For them, it means a second chance."

"You really think that's the right thing?"

"I do," Slater said, "but I'll go with whatever you think is right."

Max looked at each of them, then sighed. "OK. We'll give them an hour's head start."

Slater turned to Cash. "You can't take any of

the bogus sawbucks with you. Have you got any real money?"

"In the bedroom," he said.

"The briefcase? You have to leave that behind—the feds need to feel like they've scored a complete package. What about in a bank somewhere?"

Cash nodded. "We have other resources."

"Enough to get set up somewhere else?"

Cash looked to Logan, who nodded and said, "Yeah."

"If I unhook you," Slater said, "what are you going to do?"

"Get on the bike," Cash said, "and get as far from here as we can."

"Good," Slater said, looking at Logan, "because the feds will be here in an hour."

Slater found the kitchen knife where he'd dropped it, beside the chair Max had been tied to, and stooped beside Cash, reaching behind him and carefully cutting him free.

"Remember, I'm armed," Max said, watching as Slater grabbed Cash's hands, helping him stand up.

Slater handed Cash the knife, and he crossed the room to free Logan. Once Logan was on his feet, he went quickly to the tool cabinet and pulled out a drawer.

"He said you couldn't take anything," Max snapped.

"I'm just getting my wallet, and our passports," Logan said, holding them aloft, then stuffing them into Cash's backpack. Cash took his flute case from the far table and dropped it into the bag as well.

"I didn't think this was how things were going to turn out," Cash said to Slater. "Why are you letting us go?"

Slater eyed him. "No one is beyond redemption. Go do something honest—join a band that needs a flautist. If a package delivery guy and a hoodlum can bring you down, you know you'll get caught if you do this again. You don't want to rot in prison for half your life."

"We could have had some fun, you and me," Cash said.

"Forget all that," Slater said. "The world is full of guys. I'm the wrong one for you."

"I don't know what to say," Logan said, his erstwhile anger having evaporated, looking from Slater to Max.

"Just go," Slater demanded. "The clock is ticking."

The pair of them hustled out, closing the front door behind them.

"You know they're probably going to get picked up anyway," Max said.

"At least we gave them a fighting chance."

"Now we have to lie to the feds. That's a lot more complicated."

"So let's spend the next hour getting our story straight," Slater said.

Max stepped over to the window, looking down at the street. "Did you happen to see that briefcase full of cash in the bedroom?"

"How could I have missed it?"

"Tweedledee said it wasn't fake, but he's not exactly a reliable source."

"I believe him," Slater said. "They were only printing sawbucks, and those looked to be twenties."

"I noticed that too," Max said.

"So what are you thinking?" Slater asked.

Max moved the sheer aside with his hand, still gazing at the street. "When the feds get here, it'll go into an evidence locker, if they don't skim it for themselves. Seven years from now it'll go into the federal budget, like a grain of sand dropped on the beach."

"So nobody would miss it."

"Those boys won't be coming back for it." Max turned to look at him. "Like you said a minute ago, only if you're cool with it. We wouldn't take it all, just a percentage. We'd leave some as evidence."

"Like *you* said a minute ago, do you think that's the right thing?"

"When Mike and Jessica see their ceiling, they're never going to pay us for this job."

"We can have a look at it, at least," Slater said. "I have gloves in the car. Let's take the carpet back down on the way."

Slater stooped to roll it up, and they each took an end, carrying it down the stairs to 302 and dropping it in front of the sofa.

"Let's put it back where it was," Slater said, rolling it flat. "Fewer things to explain."

Max put the coffee table back on top of it, then went down the hallway to the bedroom to change into his suit. When he came back into the living room, he was shrugging on his jacket, his weapon where it belonged, holstered under his arm.

"Better?" Slater asked.

"It feels like all is right with the world."

"Let's be smart about this, and take our stuff out of here now."

Max handed him the delivery uniform and picked up his stepladder, still propped against the wall beside the door. Slater grabbed the chain saw and followed him out and down to the street, opening the trunk of the Thunderbird and stowing the saw, and the uniform, and his handcuffs. From the backseat he took two pairs of black latex gloves from the box he kept there, and watched from the sidewalk as Max cable-locked his ladder in the bed of the little green Courier.

Looking toward Wilshire, he wondered how far away Cash and Logan were by now.

Back in 402, they both pulled on the gloves and went into the bedroom, pulling the cash out of the briefcase to count it. It was all in twenties, and if every bundle had the same number of bills, it totaled a hundred and twelve grand.

"They're not new bills, and not in series. It's clean money," Max said finally.

"Those little monkeys," Slater said, gazing at the pile.

"Impressive, isn't it, considering sawbucks are small-time. Maybe we should go into the printing business."

"How much do we take?"

Max grinned, happy that Slater was on board. "Twenty grand each?"

"Plus twenty grand for the business. I spent a lot on all those cameras."

"What about fixing the floor?" Max said. "That'll cost another twenty."

"Deal," Slater said, and went to the kitchen, opening cupboards and drawers until he found a stash of empty plastic take-out bags, stuffing one inside another.

As they loaded up the cash, there wasn't enough room in the bag for eighty grand, and he had to go back for another set.

"It looks kind of empty," Max said, staring at the briefcase after they'd put the remaining bundles back.

"No one's going to know," Slater said, and folded it closed.

"Can you put it your car?" Max said, following him to the main room. "It'll be safer than in the Courier."

After he peeled off his gloves, Slater trotted down to the street, opening the Thunderbird's trunk and lifting the spare tire. Setting the bags of cash under it, he repositioned the tire and the chain saw, then slammed the trunk, glancing around to make sure he hadn't been observed.

Walking back up the stairs, he saw the door to 302 was open, and went to look in. Max was standing in the living room, gazing at the elegant curving staircase, covered now with rubble and a layer of plaster dust.

"Should we try to clean up?" he asked.

"The hole in the ceiling is part of our story," Slater said.

"Should we take the smoke-detector cameras down?"

"The feds probably won't find them. Even if they do, they're untraceable. They'll think Cash and Logan put them up."

Max pulled out his phone. "It's been long enough," he said, and called his contact, waiting for him to pick up, then explaining what they'd found.

"I didn't call local PD," Max said, gesturing

with his free hand, even though the person he was talking to couldn't see that. "I figured this was something for you guys. Call them in yourself if you need them." He listened, nodding. "I went in from the apartment below. … That's kind of a long story. … I unlocked the door from inside, so you can walk right in. Tread lightly, though, there are a lot of chemicals around." He recited the address, then added, "The tenants aren't around, but I'll be here, so holster your damn weapons."

Max ended the call and turned to Slater. "They'll be here soon. We might have to stick around a while longer, what with giving statements."

"Let's do one more tour of 402," Slater said, "to make sure we didn't overlook anything."

They trooped up the stairs, and next to the chair where he'd been tied, Max scooped up the plastic zip-tie handcuffs Slater had cut off him. Where Cash had been tied, Slater picked up the empty autoinjector.

"I'm glad we checked," Slater said.

There were two more pairs of plastic cuffs, the ones they'd used on Cash and Logan, and Max picked them up.

"I'll take them to the garbage chute," Max said.

"They might go through the garbage. You should put them in your truck," Slater said, and handed him the autoinjector.

"Right," Max said, and headed toward the door.

"The key," Slater said. "You told them you had it. We should leave it here on the table. That's where we found it."

Max tossed it to him before he left, and Slater set the key beside the printing press. His phone rang, and he pulled it out. It was Andy. He didn't need him anymore, now that he'd figured out what Cash was doing, and he certainly didn't need a twelve-stepper meddling in his personal life.

"What do you want?" Slater demanded, picking up.

"I want you to meet me at that … pub on Spring Street. We'll eat disgusting vegan cheesesteaks."

"I can't do it, man. I don't want to get sticky with you."

"I'm not asking you to marry me," Andy said. "Just come out for food. Everyone has to eat."

"I don't need a boyfriend," Slater said irritably.

"Neither do I. You're so freaking presumptuous. Just … show up."

"Don't tell me what to do," Slater said, but then heard noises through the hole in the floor. "Andy—hang on a second."

Stepping closer to the splintered gaping mess, he heard Jessica's voice.

"What happened in here?" she said. "Look at all the dust."

"Look at the ceiling," Mike said.

"What happened to my stuff?" Jessica said, her voice rising to a wail. "What did they do?"

Slater sighed, and stepped away, glancing out the window at the street and the bauhinias. Two black Interceptors were pulling up outside, double-parked, blue and red lights flickering faintly in the dash and the rear window. Max strolled up to greet the people who climbed out, two men from the first car, a woman from the second, all of them wearing dark suits. He couldn't hear what Max was saying, but he was waving his arms, and things looked jovial. Downstairs Jessica was screaming now, her voice reverberating but her words incomprehensible.

Rubbing his forehead, Slater spoke into his phone. "Andy, are you still there? … I'm stuck at a work thing for a couple of hours. Can we meet at the pub after that?"

Also from Dagmar Miura

That First Heady Burn

The first book in the Slater Ibáñez series sees Slater running surveillance on an injured tech worker and tangling with blackmailers, party girls, late-night hookups with a gamut of guys, and a lot of bourbon.

slater.dagmarmiura.com

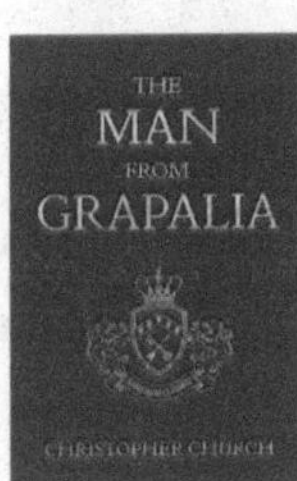

The Mason Braithwaite Paranormal Mystery Series

No one is ever quite sure whether psychic investigator Mason gets results with actual psychic power or his more mundane flatfooting, but the disheveled redhead manages to resolve some intractable mysteries.

mason.dagmarmiura.com

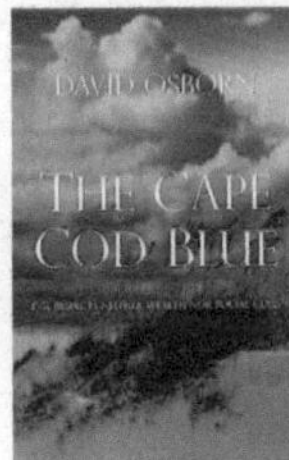

The Cape Cod Blue

The glittering, exalted world of art auctioning hides love, hate, and parricidal murder in a wealthy and socially prominent family when forgery of an anonymous Cape Cod painting is used to steal a world-famous portrait that's worth a fortune.

capecod.dagmarmiura.com

The Bone Bridge

Yarrott Benz, the 2016 Ippy Award winner for memoir, is forced to deal with extraordinary self-sacrifice in this harrowing account of teenage brothers, as different as night and day, trapped together in a dramatic medical dilemma.

bonebridge.dagmarmiura.com